THE LA~~~~~~~ ~~~~~~~

AND OTHER WRETCHED TALES

"*Despite the whimsical title, The Lamppost Huggers is a skin-crawling exercise in creeping dread, with a pitch-perfect denouement you won't see coming.*"
—Kealan Patrick Burke, Bram Stoker Award-winning author of Kin and Sour Candy

"*Christopher Stanley captures the darkness of the soul and refuses to let it go. Atmospheric and chilling, this is a true masterclass in the art of flash.*"
—Stephanie Ellis, author of Bottled

"*The Lamppost Huggers is a Pandora's box of bite-sized terror. Delightfully macabre, grotesquely disturbing and insanely original ... horror has a new name, and that is Christopher Stanley!*"
—Ross Jeffery, author of Juniper

"*Simply superb! Christopher Stanley has crafted a collection of grand vision and intimate betrayal that sweeps us from the ends of the earth to beneath our beds in terror. The Lamppost*

THE
LAMPPOST
HUGGERS
AND OTHER WRETCHED TALES

CHRISTOPHER STANLEY

THE ARCANIST PRESS
PITTSBURGH, PA

The Arcanist Press
5838 Phillips Ave APT 1
Pittsburgh, PA 15217
TheArcanist.io

Publisher's Note: This is a work of fiction. Names, characters, places, and incidents are a product of the author's imagination. Locales and public names are sometimes used for atmospheric purposes. Any resemblance to actual people, living or dead, or to businesses, companies, events, institutions, or locales is completely coincidental.

The Lamppost Huggers and Other Wretched Tales / Christopher Stanley. - 1st ed.

Cover Design by Kealan Patrick Burke / Elderlemon Design

ISBN: 978-0-578-65329-7

In loving memory of
Dorothy Mabel Stanley
"Nan"
1921-2019

CONTENTS

INTRODUCTION

I enjoyed a fortunate childhood. Perhaps there were no movies-on-demand or tens of thousands of songs in my pocket; perhaps there were only seven television channels, one of which produced wobbly, monochromatic lines during rainstorms. But on any given day (and I remain convinced the gods had a reason for this), our five-hundred-pound telly emanated a "Creature Feature" (Think: The Invisible Man, Invasion of the Body Snatchers, Roger Corman's entire filmography of B-movies complete with extra helpings of spattered fake blood).

My indulgent parents allowed me to watch them all.

Later—and by 'later' I mean the days when Mr. King was still writing as Mr. Bachman—I turned to the horror of Shirley Jackson, Roald Dahl, Richard Matheson.

Like I said, fortunate.

But there was more to come.

Jackson, Dahl, Matheson, and many other giants of the horror genre are gone, but the genre persists, rather like severed limbs that continue to regenerate, despite our best efforts to hack them off again and again. A new generation of dark fiction writers is alive and well, a band of brothers and sisters who huddle together in shadowy corners, congregate under abandoned bridges, whisper terrors in each other's ears when night descends, starless and ink-black.

The kick-ass, knock-your-socks-off, cool part? I know these people. I've met them. I've shaken their hands. Granted, I've also threatened them with poisoned doughnuts from time to time, but this seems a natural behaviour in a community of fiendishly-minded friends. And sometimes, as in this case, one of them asks me to write the introduction to his book. It's an honour I hope I'm worthy of.

Many of the stories in the collection you are about to cosy up to are fictions I've already had the pleasure of reading over the years. Many are new to me, but I recognize the deft hand of the author in their narrative. And many are stories that have sunk their teeth into my skin and refuse to let go.

There are themes running through the fictions you'll read. They range from the domestic, to the cultural to the environmental and political, even to the surreal. What binds them is their effect on us, the readers.

So, why horror? Why this fascination?

I believe there are two types of people: those who love the genre and those who have yet to understand its power. In a world chock-a-block with daily terrors (go ahead, open up a newspaper and prove me wrong on this), horror fiction affords us an escape into a different world, one where reality is put into perspective. Its message, in my mind, is always a simple one:

Relax. Things could be a hell of a lot worse.

There's a more complex relationship between the writer of horror and his reader, and the stories in this book are illustrative. Horror, when penned with the kind of insight Christopher Stanley brings to the page, is an outlet for the author's fears and a medium for transferring such fears. The following short fictions will leave you thinking about what is and what might be, what matters to us as we meander through this journey called existence. They may spur you to cuddle your children a bit longer than necessary, to look at your relationships with unveiled eyes, or even to wonder why—occasionally—one of your neighbours might be inexplicably attracted to the lamppost at the top of the street.

So read on. I'll leave you on your own to be both frightened and entertained. In my dark and stormy mind, there's little difference between the two.

Christina Dalcher
Jerez, Spain,
January, 2020

FOREWORD

Run, dear reader. Run from the darkness that creeps like bindweed across the forest floor, its spindly tendrils snapping at your ankles. Run from the noises in the canopy above your head, the cackle of magpies and the call of a carrion crow. Run from the wind that rustles the leaves like something large and unseen racing through the undergrowth. Tell yourself there's nothing there because that's what Mummy and Daddy used to tell you. There's no such thing as monsters, they'd say, it's just a blackbird foraging for worms, or a weasel or a shrew. And maybe there weren't any monsters back then, when the world was young and the days spilled over with love and joy and innocence. But you're not a child anymore, are you?

Are you afraid of witches, dear reader? Do you fear the deceitful hags who whisper strange prophesies in your ear and read your soul like the stars? Are you worried they'll hang you upside down and feed you unknown morsels while their potions boil and bubble in rust-bucket cauldrons. Does it bother you that they'll stitch their little dolls until your body isn't yours anymore? Or that they'll pin you and prick you and use your freshly spilled blood to summon demons from the darkness?

Are you afraid of the wolf? Do you fear the lycanthrope whose tormented howl can be heard in every corner of this forest, whose broken spirit can only be eased by your suffering, whose fearsome appetite can only be sated by your flesh? How do you hide from something that can smell your fear and track your scent as easily as following footprints in the snow? What hope do you have against a creature that's stronger than you and faster than you, with teeth as big as razor blades and twice as sharp? Even if it doesn't kill you, you'll never be the same again.

Or are you afraid of the wraiths? Do you fear the cold, cantankerous shades of the ones who came before you, who suffered and died before their time? Are you worried they'll surround you and suffocate you and chill you to the bone with stories of their passing? Nobody knows the dank hallways of death like those who've walked them and returned. And there are other things that linger in those hallways, as you'll soon find out.

There are monsters in this forest, dear reader. Around every corner you'll find golems and gremlins, worry dragons and worse. So come a little closer and let's brave this journey together. Run quickly and try not to make a sound. There's a way through these trees and I'm hopeful we'll find it. All you need to do is keep up.

Do you trust me?

Christopher Stanley
Bristol, England
January, 2020

THE LAMPPOST HUGGERS

AND OTHER WRETCHED TALES

CHRISTOPHER STANLEY

PART ONE

"It has long been my belief that in times of great stress, such as a 4-day vacation, the thin veneer of family wears off almost at once, and we are revealed in our true personalities."

–Shirley Jackson

NORFOLK

We arrive at the bungalow after midnight, Eddie snoring in his booster seat and Happisburgh lighthouse winking in the distance. It's exactly as I remember it from my childhood, with waves crunching beyond the dunes and the salty tang of the sea breeze. This is it, I think, as I unpack my travel-weary limbs from the car. Eccles-on-Sea, on the North Norfolk coast, is where I'm going to find the horror story that resurrects my career.

I'm supposed to be an author but I haven't sold a book in half a decade, not since my wife, Rosemary, gave birth to a boy-flavoured bundle of toothless smiles and Godless nappies. Eddie wasn't planned and it's hard not to blame him for my aborted career. The only reason I brought him with me is because Rosemary insisted I learn to write with him in the room. I tried to argue, pleading the need for authorial solitude, but he's here and she's not.

Half of Eccles was stolen by the sea some centuries ago and what's left is barely a ghost town. They say a storm once shifted so much sand from the beach it uncovered the old graveyard, tearing open coffins and scattering skeletons up the coast. "With history like that," said Rosemary, "who needs horror?"

I fall asleep listening to the wind tugging at the dunes. In my dreams, the spirits of the dead crawl from the water to steal Eddie away, their fleshless fingers prising him from my grasp. I'm glad they're taking him but I'm compelled to ask why. One word comes hissing back:

"Innocent."

I'm startled into consciousness by something clawing at my face. When I switch on the bedside light, Eddie's on top of me, saying he had a nightmare in which hollow-eyed ghosts crossed the dunes and descended on our bungalow. "They took me away from you," he whispers, unaware of how similar our dreams were.

Outside, the shed creaks in the wind while rain pelts the windows. And there's something else, something more deliberate. I hold Eddie tight, telling him there are no ghosts, only stories, but something is thumping the walls of the bungalow. The look on Eddie's face says it all. The spirits have come for him; our dreams are coming true.

"I'll try not to let them get you, Eddie."

"You have to!"

For a moment, I'm confused, but then I remember that Eddie woke me up mid-dream. "In your nightmare," I say, "where did the ghosts take you?"

"To the safe place."

And now I understand. It isn't rain hitting the windows; it's spray from the rising sea. The thumping sound is water. Somewhere in the bungalow a window shatters, and then another. The two halves of Eccles are going to be reunited, tonight. I cling desperately to Eddie, promising him I'll never let go.

"I'll miss you, Daddy," he says, as shadows gather in the hallway. "But I'll tell everyone what happened and I'm sure they'll buy your books again."

WHISTLE-STOP

Banff National Park

Selina and Jake fly into Calgary for a driving tour of Western Canada that will eventually take them to Vancouver, where her husband is speaking at the TED Conference. Years have passed since her last real holiday and she's looking forward to spending time with her seven-year-old son. Their first stop is the postcard-perfect Banff, with its green-velvet pine trees and turquoise meltwaters. They walk along the river and Selina slips off her sandals to let the icy water nip at her toes. On their hotel balcony, she basks in the sunset and sips a native Pinot Noir, while Jake plays 80's arcade games on his tablet.

Jasper National Park

Jake doesn't always play the games. Sometimes, he's distracted by the simple beauty of the graphics and stops playing to watch. Selina's learned to accept his peculiarities. The way he always seems to know what song they'll play next on the radio, or when her husband's about to walk through the front door. She remembers how, on his first day at school, he insisted on taking a raincoat and wellies, even though the long, dry summer showed no signs of cooling. That lunchtime he was the only child allowed out to play in the muddy puddles.

After the majestic mountains and whipped cream glaciers of the Icefields Parkway, Jasper seems uninspiring. Jake watches Tetris without ever touching the screen, and Selina is bored. She wants to know if its dinnertime yet but, like Jake, the clock on the wall seems to have given up.

Wells Gray Provincial Park

In their cagoules, they watch the Chinook salmon leaping up the rapids. Between the rustle of their raincoats and the water splatting down from the tree canopy, Selina wonders if they would hear an approaching grizzly before they were savaged. For nearly an hour, Jake counts the salmon while she sings nursery rhymes out loud because she read in a book it's best to let bears know where you are.

Jake plays Frogger while she puts their waterproofs in the boot of their rental car. Through the rear window, she sees the famed arcade frog sitting at the side of the road, waiting to cross. Just waiting and waiting. She collapses into the driver's seat and turns the keys in the ignition, but the car won't start. She turns it again, still worrying about bears and praying she won't have to call for help. Annoyed, she tells Jasper to either play his game or switch the damn thing off. The next time she turns the keys, the engine rumbles to life quite happily.

Whistler

The snow descends like some biblical swarm as they trudge up the mountain to the cable car station. They set off nervously and even the little red gondola shudders. Seven passengers, including Selina, stare silently out of the windows as the ground falls away. Jake sits on a wooden bench and plays Space Invaders, the chirp of the laser cannon punctuating the mechanical grumble of pulleys running over cable. For a few minutes, it seems like they're flying hundreds of metres above the tops of the pine trees, and then the world disappears. Selina turns full circle, searching through the windows for anything with a hard edge, but all she can see is the mist. Somebody laughs nervously and an old man with a walking stick says 'Is it true this is the longest, unsupported cable car in the world?'

Jake starts another game. With a jolt, the cable car stops moving, the gondola rocking backwards and forwards. Selina looks for an explanation but all she can see in any direction is a few metres of cable disappearing into nothing. The other passengers shuffle uneasily. The old man asks 'Is this normal?' No, thinks Selina. Normal is two feet on solid ground. Normal is a glass of wine and a hot bath after Jake's gone to bed.

Remembering her son, she looks over and sees him sitting on his hands, watching while the aliens do their colourful dance down the screen. He seems happy enough but she feels more anxious than ever. 'We'll be going again in no time,' says the old man with a reassuring nod. 'I hear that lunch on Blackcomb Mountain is worth hanging around for.'

While the other tourists snicker politely, Selina checks her watch and remembers the clock on the wall in Jasper—how it stopped ticking when Jake stopped playing Tetris. She remembers the car not starting in Wells Gray. She looks at Jake's tablet and can't help noticing the laser canon's shape is remarkably similar to the shape of their gondola. She feels her chest tighten as the aliens descend. What happens when the aliens reach the bunkers? What happens when they reach the laser canon?

'Jake,' she says. 'Play properly.'

Jake smiles as the aliens slice through the roofs of the bunkers.

'Jake,' she says again. 'Play the game or switch it off.'

The old man puts his hand on her elbow. 'Let the boy be,' he says.

'But he's not playing.'

'He's all right.'

On the screen, the bunkers have already been halved.

'You don't understand,' says Selina. 'If he doesn't play, we're all going to…' She stops and looks at the other passengers, feeling stupid and confused.

Trying to remain calm, she stares back out of the window and jumps when something flashes past above them. The mist swirls like smoke in a breeze and she's sure she can hear a faint hum. She touches her fingers to the glass and feels it vibrating. There's something up there. Something big, and fast. She looks at the other passengers, wanting to warn them but unsure what to say. The hum grows louder and more threatening. Again, something passes through the mist above their heads. This time it's close enough to rattle the gondola.

On Jake's tablet, the aliens dismantle the last of the bunkers.

The end is imminent.

The screen flashes.

Game over.

BOLESKINE

Rain falls helter-skelter before skittering across the murky waters of Loch Ness. Something big ripples towards the south-eastern shore. There are monsters here, numerous documented sightings, but the creature emerging from the shallows is broadly that of a middle-aged woman, save for a lingering tail and serpentine tongue. A stray cat hops up onto a gravestone and she breaks its neck, offering it up to Hecate before biting into its abdomen. Blood slithers down her torso and is washed away by the rain until the only remaining trace of the monster is a note of displeasure in the turn of her lips.

Beyond the cemetery, a single-storey manor house glows in the moonlight. She remembers calling its name, over and over, the word sounding familiar and foreign at the same time. Boleskine. As she approaches, the iron gates part and flames dance excitedly in the lanterns on either side of the door. Boleskine never returned her calls, not until today.

"Welcome home, my darling rosebud."

His voice comes from both ends of the hallway simultaneously. She should have known better than to imagine he was dead; the rules of mortality have never held firm in this part of Scotland. She hears a baby crying and follows the sound into the sitting room, using an oil lamp to light her way. In the middle of the floor there's a mahogany drinks cabinet, standing tall on claw and ball feet. As she approaches, the doors open to display decanters full of amber escapism and regiments of lead crystal glasses. Her mouth is suddenly dry like the Egyptian desert of her honeymoon.

"You always had weakness for alcohol."

It's been decades since she drank anything other than water from the loch. She touches a glass and it shatters, as does the one next to it. A decanter cracks, sloshing its contents onto the carpet. She steps backwards as the other glasses explode into a million tiny shards. And then the cabinet starts to twist and buckle.

She leaves the room quickly and follows the sound of crying into the dining room. The far wall is covered in oil paintings, five of them, arranged on the points of a pentagram. She reads the names underneath each painting. Mary d'Este Sturges, Jeanne Robert Foster, Roddie Minor, Marie Rohling and Leah Hirsig. She doesn't recognise the names but she knows who they were. His scarlet women, his sacred whores. In the centre of the pentagram is a mirror and in the mirror is a face that hasn't changed in nearly a century.

"You drove me into the arms of other lovers."

Once again she follows the sound of crying, this time into a bedroom decorated with rose-patterned wallpaper. On a sheepskin rug, a cot rocks gently. There's a name engraved into the side panel. Lilith. She approaches the cot, not daring to breathe, hoping against reason for a glimpse of her little girl. But when she steps on the rug, the crying stops. The cot is empty.

"You let our daughter die."

Blinded by tears, she flees the room, tripping and nearly falling through the door. The flickering flame of her oil lamp makes a carnival of the walls. As she steadies herself she sees something shift in the gloom at the end of the hallway. A tall, robed figure emerges from the shadows, antlers sprouting from its oversized head.

"I hated you, Rose Edith Kelly. That's why I made you a monster. That's why I condemned you to the loch."

The creature removes its headpiece, revealing the round, hairless face of her former husband, Aleister Crowley.

"How would you like to see Lilith again?" he asks. "Together we could bring her back."

There's nothing Rose wants more. Nothing she's ever wanted more. Crowley beckons her to join him and she steps forward, shivering as his hands slip over her hips.

"My mother called me 'the Beast'," he says, "and I made you a monster. But you don't have to be a monster anymore. I've forgiven you."

He pulls her closer until she, too, is engulfed by his black velvet robes and the familiar scents of hashish and sex and magick. She can't remember the last time she felt needed or desired. But she's been here before. While they were married, Crowley exposed her to all manner of madness until she turned to drink. He told her he loved her but he cheated on her and filed for divorce. He dragged her to every unclean corner of the world until their daughter died of typhoid in her arms.

"Let me set you free," he says. "I've been so lonely without you."

Rose lifts the oil lamp up to his face and raises her lips to his ear. "You always made such fantastic promises," she whispers, wondering how quickly his tattered robe would burn. "But I like being a monster."

***

On her way back to the loch, she pauses by a moss-covered headstone and kneels to pay her respects. Boleskine never answered her calls before and it never would again. But sometimes, when she surfaced for air, she could hear a child crying on the south-eastern shore.

Her daughter, Lilith. Waiting.

GETTYSBURG

An American robin perches high up on the corner of the Pennsylvania State Memorial, twitching his head this way and that to observe the field below. As the raw, morning sun chases whorls of mist to the horizon, he sees earthworms churning up the field with their fat, writhing bodies. Millions of them. Morning hungry, the robin doesn't know where to feed first. Only when he senses the arrival of other birds does he flap down for his breakfast.

At the top of the memorial steps, Maia and her grandmother hold the leather-bound book between them and read aloud. They aren't dressed to draw attention. Maia's blonde bob brushes against the collar of her gilet; her grandmother's burnt-charcoal plait is tied with a bow of black ribbon below the waist of her jeans. If it weren't for the look of murder in Maia's eyes, they could almost be tourists.

Hard as the robin pulls, the earthworm won't yield. Other birds flutter down in their thousands to join the feast. Cowbirds and red-winged blackbirds see-saw as they try to prise their prey from the ground. Slowly, they all sink into the mud. The robin's beak disappears and then his head. He flaps his wings uselessly until the air is gone from his lungs.

Maia's voice grows louder and more determined as other predators arrive. Cats and snakes snap their teeth into the dying birds, only to find that they, too, start sinking. They struggle and thrash but soon the field is still. Not for the first time, Cemetery Ridge in Gettysburg National Military Park reeks of death.

And then something pushes up through the ground, rising above the carnage.

An arm, a head, a wing.

***

Maia was already annoyed as she waited for her grandmother outside the Adams County Courthouse. Above her head, the American flag struggled against the wind, a reminder of what was at stake. In recent months she'd marched in support of minority groups and offered pro bono representation to immigrants and refugees. She told herself things couldn't get any worse but every day they did. And now her grandmother had summoned her to Gettysburg. She didn't want to be here, there was too much to do back in Boston and she hated leaving Fatemah behind, but the note said to come urgently.

"Have you been practicing?" asked her grandmother as they entered the courthouse. "Of course you haven't. Not since your parents passed away. Not that they let you practice before."

Maia followed her grandmother through room after room, from floor to floor, until they ended up in a mildewed cupboard lit by a naked tungsten bulb. On the wall was a single oak shelf containing a dust-furred, leather-bound book called 'American Incantations.' Her grandmother licked her fingers and flicked through the pages until she arrived at a chapter called 'Gettysburg.'

"Read," she said.

At first Maia was distracted by the blood-speckled lettering, but soon the phrases began to seem familiar. "…a new nation, conceived in Liberty … engaged in a great civil war … from these honoured dead … to that cause for which they gave the last full measure of devotion…"

She raised her eyebrows. "The Gettysburg Address was a spell?"

"Read on."

Later in her hotel room, she fidgeted angrily on the bed. She wanted to speak to Fatemah, to be soothed by her lover's voice, but the phone line was busy. What her grandmother was proposing was unconscionable. "We'll keep protesting," Maia had argued. "It's better to fight them in the courts than the streets." But her grandmother believed the time for peaceful protest was over. The spell was their only hope.

She turned on the television, only to be confronted with images of a mosque being squeezed by fingers of fire. She closed her eyes and prayed for sleep, but the news wouldn't go away. Stories of Muslims detained in holding pens, awaiting deportation. The virulent spread of racially-motivated murders and the savage retort of the firing squad. Bodies hung from lampposts or dragged bleeding through the streets. And Fatemah. Sweet Fatemah. With her cocoa eyes and vanilla lips, Fatemah was the only thing that made sense in the world. Maia watched as her lover was stripped, beaten and bound atop a burning pyre of hate and censored literature. She woke up screaming Fatemah's name and vomited until only darkness remained inside her.

"You read the spell," her grandmother said, her black silk dressing gown flapping like the wings of a bat. "It's shown you the future."

"They burned her like a witch. We must stop them. We must crush them now."

Her grandmother smiled. And nodded.

***

On Cemetery Ridge, Maia watches the creature unfolding towards the sky. It stands at least ten feet tall; a man-shaped monster of mud and feather and bone. His head twitches this way and that as fifty thousand others just like him rise up from the ground.

"The golems of Gettysburg," says Maia.

"If this doesn't work," says her grandmother, "they'll come for us. They'll know what we are."

The creatures take to the sky, their wings pounding like canon fire as they fly south to Washington and the White House.

"It'll work," says Maia. "And we shall harvest the bones of everyone who stands opposed to democracy, to freedom, to the idea of an America for all. Pennsylvania Avenue will run red with the blood of the unworthy. For we are many, we are unstoppable and we are coming."

ABSENT SPOUSE SYNDROME

"Daddy isn't coming anymore," calls Sarah down the stairs. "He has a migraine."

On the bedroom floor, Nigel's body lies limp and lifeless on a rug, his copper hair matted with blood and fragments of bone where she hit him with the nine iron. The early morning sun sends shadows across the carpet, reaching like fingers to steal his corpse into the darkness. Sarah drops the club and sits on the edge of the bed, her arms still shaking from the impact. There's nothing she can do now except pack the suitcases in the car and go. Kaitlin won't be happy about leaving her dad behind but a week's holiday on the Devonshire coast is exactly what they both need. With Nigel gone, Sarah can listen to One Direction in the car and eat any flavour of Pringles she wants. And no one is going to repack her holiday bags ever again.

Under a blue and white polka dot sky, they make daily trips to the beach, play crazy golf and sunbathe by the pool. In their chalet, they wear tiger-stripe onesies and paint their toenails all the colours of the rainbow. But the days fall from the calendar until it's time for Sarah to start forcing souvenirs into her suitcase, which she does with a creeping sense of dread. What will they find when they arrive home? A stinking corpse? A houseful of flies? And what will she say to Kaitlin? She almost hopes they'll discover their home swaddled in crime scene tape. A hostile interrogation at the station would be vastly preferable to the alternative: sawing up her husband's body and dividing it between heavy duty refuse sacks.

Back home, she sends Kaitlin to search for her dad in the study while she lugs the suitcase up to the bedroom, preparing for the worst. Will there be rats? Will his skin be the colour of fallen leaves? Will it be the *texture* of fallen leaves? She holds her breath and lets the door swing open.

Nigel isn't there. His body is gone. Only the nine iron and the bloodstained rug remain.

"Where's Daddy?" asks Kaitlin when Sarah returns from the bedroom.

"I really don't know."

That night, while Kaitlin sleeps, Sarah bleaches the golf club and rolls the rug into the boot of her car. With a kitchen knife trembling in her hand, she searches the house, half-expecting Nigel's cadaver to jump out at her. When she's run out of places to look, she drops the knife to the floor, collapses into a chair and sobs.

Where is he?

For years she's wanted him out of her life but this is going too far. Why can't he just be dead like any normal person? In bed, she lies awake, examining the silence for footsteps, her eyes daring the bedroom door to open. It seems too much to hope that his body has evaporated, absorbed into the atmosphere and dispersed by draft and breeze. But that's how her father went. One day he was there, and the next her mum was popping sleeping pills and claiming she was cursed.

***

At the weekend, Sarah takes Kaitlin to the Marriott Royal Hotel in Bristol, dressing it up as a girl's night out. Since Nigel's body disappeared, she's changed the locks on every door and installed video monitors in the hall, stairs and landing, but she hasn't been able to sleep at all. Every time Kaitlin gets up to use the loo, she's convinced it's Nigel coming back to kill her. By the end of the week, she's so exhausted she's started snoozing next to the photocopier in work and dozing through multiple laps of the bus route. One afternoon she woke up in the magazine aisle of the local supermarket, her cheek imprinted with a fragment of newspaper headline. When she looked in the mirror, the text just said, "Murderer."

But it's going to be okay.

The moment they step into the marble and mahogany reception area of the hotel, she feels calmer, safer. Nothing can hurt them in this beautiful, bustling fortress for the living. And she knows a good night's sleep will cure everything.

While Kaitlin changes for dinner, Sarah freshens up in the bathroom. She studies her refection in the mirror, her face telling the story of her age and anxieties in a thousand unwanted lines. After she's showered, she brushes her hair and cleans her teeth, but the toothbrush feels all wrong in her mouth. When she looks she realises it isn't hers; it's Nigel's. She returns to the bedroom to tell Kaitlin, only to find her daughter sitting with the nine iron on her lap.

"What are you doing?"

"Is this Daddy's?"

"Why did you bring that?"

"I didn't," says Kaitlin. "You did."

That night, she lies awake for hours, worrying her daughter is colluding with her dead husband. She revisits their conversations and retraces their footsteps to see if she's missed something important. When she does sleep, she dreams that Nigel is in their hotel room, blood and tissue oozing from the hole in his head. She tries to explain why she killed him but he won't let her finish her sentences. She opens her eyes in shock and he's on top of her, hands around her throat, eyes glistening with madness. Kaitlin's screaming and something is banging against the door, thumping and thumping.

"Mummy! Stop it!"

The door opens and the room rearranges itself the way they always do upon waking. Nigel is gone, and Sarah is on Kaitlin's bed, her thumbs pressed against her daughter's windpipe.

Standing in the doorway, the hotel security guard sees everything.

OYMYAKON

The priest's backhanded slap caught me hard on the cheekbone and my head twisted around with such force I thought he'd broken my neck. That bastard. He thumbed something cold against my forehead and mumbled a prayer I couldn't hear over the ringing in my ears. Red-eyed and spittle-toothed, he looked quite wretched as he sat there, straddling me on the bed. Judging by the stench of piss and vomit that encircled us like a graveyard fog, I probably looked worse. The priest lifted the silver cross from my forehead and touched it to his lips. He said the demon was gone but a monster remained. I spat blood in his face, accusing him of fake news, of failure to move on. He said if I loved my family, I'd get as far away from them as possible.

Afterwards, I tried to act normal but my wife refused to leave me alone with our daughters. A fortnight passed before I was allowed back in our bedroom and even then she wouldn't let me see her naked, saying the way I looked at her made her uncomfortable. While she slept, I kissed the back of her neck where it curves into her shoulder and remembered the promises we made to each other on our wedding day. Then I licked my lips to savour the salty-sweet taste of her skin.

The night I bit her she said I had to go.

The priest offered me a place to stay if I moved to Oymyakon, in the Sakha Republic of Russia. The coldest turning off the Road of Bones. The video showed an attractive young woman throwing a pan of freshly-boiled water into the air before disappearing into her own, private blizzard. The truth is less glamorous. Everyone shits in a shed outside because it's too cold for plumbing. Mobile phones don't work and we all live on a diet of horsemeat because crops won't grow.

Horsemeat.

Before the demon, I used to enjoy homemade American meatloaf. Lobster and shrimp in my favourite restaurant. Now everything tastes like tofu with a side of nothing. The priest was right, the demon is gone but a monster remains.

And it's hungry.

In moonlight, I head for the funeral home. Nobody gets buried quickly in Oymyakon because it takes three days to thaw the ground enough to dig a grave. I watch through the windows, waiting for a corpse to be left unattended, but it's like they know I'm here.

There's no playground at the school. Even in fur-lined coats and scarves, it would be dangerous for the kids to play outside. Parents march their offspring through the main entrance and I wonder if my daughters miss me. They had big eyes and the smoothest, tenderest skin. The children in Oymyakon look like they've been dressed to minimise temptation.

"I know what you are," says a voice behind me. I spin around, equally alarmed and surprised. I haven't heard anyone speak English since I arrived. The old man introduces himself as Ivan Kuznetsov and says, "There's something I need to show you."

***

"My name is Abenayo," says the Ghanaian woman behind the lectern, "and I'm recovering from demonic possession."

Kuznetsov isn't here but this is what he wanted to show me. Fifty seats facing a modest stage. A room full of shadows on the edge of town.

"My husband was a doctor," says Abenayo, "He worked in the same hospital as my sister." She swallows hard, clutching her cardigan like she doesn't trust the buttons. "I still don't know who seduced who."

The seats are filled with men and women from all over the world. Most of us speak English. Some don't.

"I prayed to God," she says. "But it wasn't God who answered."

Before I killed him, Kuznetsov told me that Oymyakon is where they send the survivors. The support group was his idea. He wanted to help us recover.

"I burned my sister's house while she was asleep," says Abenayo. "Then I burned the hospital. After that, I burned everything I could. It felt so … right."

Abenayo doesn't look like she's recovering. As she unbuttons her cardigan and unzips her jeans, she looks like she'd burn this whole fucking place down, given half a chance.

"At first I just washed my feet in it," she says, her clothes falling down around her ankles. "More recently, I've taken baths." Stripped to her underwear, her skin is half boiled from her body. Angry welts explode like fireworks across her chest. "Bathing in gasoline," she says, "is almost as good as the burn."

Nobody gasps. Nobody looks away. We're all monsters here; Abenayo's the only one who's honest enough to wear it on the outside.

When it's my turn to speak, I don't tell them my name. My human name is irrelevant. "The priest who exorcised my demon," I say, "he took something from me. Something important." Around the room, heads bob in agreement. "Nobody asked me what I wanted. Nobody cared about me. And now I'm here, and I'm pissed, and I'm hungry."

The audience responds with enthusiastic grunts and I can feel something rising inside me. I'm Martin Luther King on the steps of the Lincoln Memorial. Al Pacino in City Hall.

"I want my demon back," I say.

"Yes."

I slam my fist onto the lectern. "I want my demon back!"

"Yes!"

"Say it!"

"I want my demon back."

"Say it louder!"

"I want my demon back!"

"If we burn their houses."

"Yes!"

"If we sacrifice the innocent."

"Yes! Yes!"

"We can bring the fires of hell to Oymyakon!"

Kuznetsov didn't fight me. Tied to a chair in my back room, he understood this was always his fate. As I chewed on his severed fingers and peeled long strips of flesh from his body, he said he knew it was only a matter of time.

He'd hoped to make us better. But it's just too cold for hope in Oymyakon.

CHILDREN OF THE MOON

Another empty desk in the classroom. Cop cars in the playground and hushed voices in the corridors. My classmates sit with their heads down, hair spiked defensively, while a doughnut-shaped cop talks of curfews and counselling. When it's my turn to be interrogated, I tell her I'm new to the area. I say I didn't know the missing kids. She looks suspicious.

We moved to the Jersey shore three weeks ago, Mum and me. I was just beginning to feel like I could fit in when children started disappearing. I guess it won't be long before we're leaving again.

When a third child disappears, plucked in darkness from the highest seat on the Ferris wheel, Bobby corners me in the toilets. Elbow crushing my windpipe, he wants to know what I'm going to do. "Round here," he says, "we take care of our own." Before I can reply, he's scratched my palm and pressed his freshly-bitten thumb into the wound. "You're one of us now."

Later, we gather in the moonlight outside Krueger's discount video store. Fifteen of us. I study their faces, thinking how young and innocent they look, even as they speak of monsters.

"I heard he's a biter," says Skeeter.

"No reflection," says Rowlf. "No soul."

"The monster is not a 'he'," says Bobby. "And *she's* getting sloppy." I gasp with the others when he holds up a broken necklace—a chunky silver choker with fake sapphires. They take turns to sniff it and lick it with pointed tongues, and then drift towards the darkness with their noses in the air. I watch their moon-shadows as they leave, hunched forward, knees bending, knuckles dragging along the ground. I watch until they're walking on all-fours.

Like evolution in reverse.

And my skin is tingling. I'm changing too. Mum'll kill me if she finds me with this lot, but I have to get her necklace back.

JEREMY'S WISH

England on a Christmas morning looks nothing like the acres of snow-covered fields and frost-dusted trees depicted on greetings cards. The world outside the French windows is the same as it's been all month. A light drizzle hangs in the air, muting the color of everything except the algae on the fence panels. Cobwebs decorate the conifers and cat poo covers the lawn. Jeremy stares up into the colorless, magic-less sky, thinking that if the Christmas cards are a lie, could the boys at school have been right about Santa Claus?

In the living room, there are gifts all around the tree—a rolling landscape of prettily wrapped parcels that weren't there when Jeremy went to bed the previous evening. Rob, his dad, says the pile of presents is obscene. Most of them are modest offerings—packages no bigger than a man's knitted sweater—but at the back of the room, standing upright against the wall, there's a parcel that's taller than the tree. The label reads "To Jeremy from Santa."

"What did you buy him?" asks Linda, Jeremy's mum, looking puzzled.

"Don't look at me," says Rob. "You're the one who doesn't know when to stop."

After breakfast, Rob smokes a cigarette on the porch while Jeremy helps his mum sort out the presents, trying to guess what they might be. This is Jeremy's favorite time. In the minutes before the first presents are opened it seems like anything might be possible. The moment is spoiled when Rob returns, lumbering into the room like an arthritic dinosaur and saying "Let's get this over with."

The three of them rip the paper from their presents, liberating packs of socks, box sets of DVDs and cartons of sweets. Linda's main present is underwear, although she calls it "lingerie", pronouncing the word with a funny accent and a playful smile. Rob's main present is a home-brew kit. "What the fuck am I supposed to do with this?" he asks as he unpacks a thermometer, a bung and a large glass jar called a demijohn. Linda rolls her eyes and shakes her head, but not enough for Rob to notice.

"Why don't you open your main present, sweetie?" she says to Jeremy.

Jeremy carefully removes the paper from his main present to reveal an upright timber crate.

"Goal posts for the garden, maybe?" says Linda.

"A fruit machine for his bedroom?" suggests Rob.

Anticipation tickles the insides of Jeremy's tummy as he prises open the latch and swings the lid wide.

He gasps. Maybe Christmas is magic after all.

The man who steps out of the crate looks exactly the way Rob would look if he spent less time at the pub and more time at the gym. Jeremy stares at the man's bulgeless waist and taut chin, wondering how someone can be so familiar and so alien at the same time. The man squats down so he's Jeremy's height and the smell of his aftershave makes Jeremy feel giddy. "You must be Jeremy," he says, smiling like he means it. "I'm going to be your new daddy."

"What is this?" asks Rob. "Some kind of joke? I'm calling the Police!"

"Wait," says Jeremy. "Don't." He stares at Rob, an anxious feeling expanding against his chest. Speaking too quickly, he says, "You said I couldn't have an Xbox for Christmas so I asked Santa for ... a new dad instead."

The room is still. The clock ticks in the kitchen. Somewhere the central heating whoomphs to life. And Jeremy wonders if this is it, if these are the last sounds he will ever hear. Then Rob shoves the new dad into the Christmas tree, which jingles and snaps as both it and the new dad collapse on the floor. "Where's my phone?" asks Rob, swiping balls of wrapping paper from the arms of the sofa in his frustration. He's about to call the Police when the new dad climbs out of the Christmas tree, picks up the five-litre demijohn and smashes it over the back of Rob's head. The demijohn explodes in a firework of glass and bloodied hair, and Rob stumbles forward, falling flat on his face.

The new dad stands over Rob with a six-inch shard of broken glass in his hand. "You should probably look away," he says to Jeremy and Linda.

Jeremy closes his eyes and cuddles into his mum's shoulder. For the next few minutes he hears strangled pleas and desperate sobs followed by stabbing, squelching and splattering noises. Jeremy flinches with each new sound, feeling every slash and blow. And then there's only silence.

"You can look now," says the new dad, panting lightly.

Jeremy and Linda peer out from behind their hands. Lying in the centre of the room, covered in crimson fingerprints, is the crate in which the new dad arrived. The carpet and walls are covered in violent arcs of blood, all dripping towards the carpet.

"It's okay," says the new dad. "Most of it's his."

Linda leaps off the sofa and runs for the door in panic, but the new dad catches her, wrapping his strong arms around her chest. "You can't run away," he says, his voice little more than a whisper. "We're all going to stay here and celebrate Christmas together." She falls to her knees and sobs quietly, gently rocking backwards and forwards next to the blood-smeared crate.

"I almost forgot," says the new dad, handing Jeremy a Christmas present. Jeremy's eyes light up as he unwraps what turns out to be a brand new Xbox. "I'm sure your mum won't mind," says the new dad. "And if she does, we'll know who to get you for your birthday."

Jeremy looks past his new dad towards the world beyond the French windows. The drizzle has stopped and the first precious flakes of snow are dancing in the sky. It's been a marvellous Christmas. He can't wait to tell his friends all about it.

.

HEART OF STONE

David placed the present on Monica's bedside table and told her to open it after he'd gone home. His lips kept moving but she could no longer hear what he was saying over the pounding of her heart. Was this it? Was this his idea of a proposal? When it was time for him to leave, she watched him breeze past the queue of mums pushing babies in plastic trollies, and then ripped off the wrapping paper. Inside the gaudy display wallet was a sliver of moon rock, speckled and grey and about the size of a diamond ring.

But it wasn't a ring.

After she returned home from the maternity ward, David complained about the cost of nappies and Emma's constant crying. He moaned about loss of sleep and the disruption to their routines. Monica tried to remember how he was when they first met, when their love was liquid and explosive. Two nights later, David moved into the spare room.

"Maybe if you hold Emma," she said. "Let her get used to you." Emma was on her back, plump and wrinkled like a balled-up sock, her feet kicking the air.

David's reply was a stone-cold stare.

Standing at the nursery window, Monica sang lullabies while staring up at the stars. She listened to David's distant snoring and tried to imagine what it would be like to have a good night's sleep. Afterwards, she slipped into bed with him and tried to cuddle into his warmth. Every time she touched him, he moved further away.

The following morning, David limped downstairs for breakfast, complaining that his legs were so stiff he could barely stand up. Half-drunk with tiredness and the aroma of baby lotion, Monica watched him from the lounge, Emma cooing contentedly in her arms. David finished his cereal in silence and didn't even say goodbye when he left for work.

While he was gone, Monica introduced Emma to her display of precious rocks and minerals. Tucked into the corner of her bedroom were shelves of amethyst clusters, Bristol diamonds and jasper thundereggs—exquisite beauty born from the fires of volcanoes and rhyolite lava flows. She'd hoped the moon rock might fill the gap in her collection, but there was still something missing. It didn't matter. Emma smiled for the first time ever and it seemed as though sunshine poured from her face.

While Emma slept, Monica slipped the moonrock from its case and ran it between her fingers. It was cold, hard and inconsequential. She tried to imagine a world where David gave her a diamond ring instead, but it didn't seem real. She closed her eyes, rubbed her fingers over the rock and wished things were different.

At three o'clock, David phoned to say he'd be working late. He did this most days but usually it came with a half-hearted apology. Monica was in bed by the time he arrived home. She listened to him grunt up the stairs. When he appeared in the bedroom doorway, his complexion was greyer than granite. She offered to make him an appointment with the doctor, but he shook his head.

"It's this house," he said. "I'm fine while I'm at work."

She touched her hand to his forehead and he jerked away from her.

"I'm not sick."

"Would you like to hold your daughter?" she asked. "A cuddle might help."

"That's all I need," he replied. "More weight to carry. No thank you."

That night, for the first time since he'd moved back into the main bedroom, David didn't disturb her with his snoring. He didn't steal the covers or wedge his knee into the small of her back.

Monica dreamed she was flying through the swirling colours of the cosmos, past distant stars and galaxies, until she rained back down to Earth in a thousand slivers of moon rock. She didn't wake up until she heard David's radio alarm.

"Morning," she said, rolling over for a cuddle.

But David wasn't there.

She sat up, fumbling for the bedside light switch, wincing as the room lit up. Then she pulled the covers back to see what was lying next to her.

David's pyjamas.

David's shape.

David's skin turned to stone.

"Help ... me," he whispered.

"Oh my God. David?"

"Must ... go."

He rolled out of bed, his body thumping against the floor hard enough to rattle her display of precious rocks and minerals. Grimacing, he hauled himself towards the bedroom door. "Can't ... be ... here."

She watched him trying to leave and almost felt sorry for him. She wondered what was happening to him, thinking it must be some sort of skin disease or allergic reaction. She reached for her phone to call the emergency services, but couldn't bring herself to dial. As David inched across the floor, she pressed her foot down between his shoulders and said, "No."

David's skin was coarse like concrete and his joints were reluctant to cooperate, but still she managed to haul him back onto the bed, propping him up against the headboard. Panting hard, she said "We need to talk."

She told him he had to do better. He needed to spend more time at home with her and Emma. She said he'd brought this on himself.

When she was finished, she fetched Emma from the nursery and nestled her in David's arms. Emma's eyes shone the way David's used to—the rich, deep blue of lapis lazuli. Tearful, she watched her daughter giggle as her little fingers reached up to stroke David's chin.

Before Monica left the maternity ward, she'd imagined a future of family portraits, birthday parties, and ice cream faces at the beach. She'd dreamed of an engagement ring with a diamond that sparkled like distant stars. And maybe these things could still happen. For now, it was enough her family were all together.

Finally, her collection felt complete. And it was precious.

PART TWO

"I searched everywhere for a proof of reality, when all the while I understood quite well that the standard of reality had changed."

–Algernon Blackwood

WICKED COLLABORATION

Eleanor sits like a tombstone in the early morning silence of her car, cloaked in creeping vines of fear. Outside the world is as it's always been. Light falls from distant stars and mist floats like a ghost upon the breeze. Inside the car, everything has changed. Beneath the rear-view mirror, where last week she'd hung a cardboard air freshener in the shape of a pine tree, there's now a bright orange pumpkin—a goofily grinning jack-o'-lantern toy with black triangle eyes and a tiny body made from beads and elastic. She stares at it suspiciously, her fingers clenched into fists, her breath catching in her throat. The jack-o'-lantern is a mark of mischief and she's afraid of what it might mean.

"Trick or treat," she mutters with an accent that hints at ancient woodlands and faraway places. "Treats and tricks!" She twists the car key a third time, counting one second, two seconds, three, but the engine refuses to start. Instead, she hears the sound again; a muffled, wayward snigger on the other side of the dashboard. She exits the vehicle in a hurry, leaving her keys swinging from the ignition as she rushes up the rain-dampened path towards the high street, the bus stop, the bus.

"Wait!"

On board, the seats are already taken and the air is close to boiling. The ageing bus creaks away from the kerb and lurches unsteadily towards the city centre, growling like the belly of a dragon, screeching to a stop at every set of red lights. The other passengers giggle and chatter as though the world isn't ending. She stares at their faces but all she sees is the horror that might be unfolding in the maternity ward because she isn't there.

When the bus eventually shudders to a halt outside the hospital, the doors don't move. Eleanor clenches her fists, fear squeezing her gut, certain the creatures are planning to hold her captive. Her eyes flick from the exit to the driver, waiting for a reaction, wondering why he's just sitting there. Has he been charmed? Then the doors snap open and she's slapped in the face by a rush of cold air. She leaves quickly and doesn't look back.

The hospital throbs like an industrial heart. The maternity ward is on wrong side of the building furthest from the bus stop. She holds her ID pass in her hand but every security door takes a moment too long to open. Friends and colleagues weigh her down with sunny greetings and expectant faces; unwittingly aiding the mischief that's already permeating the hospital corridors.

Can't they sense it?

Everywhere she looks, there are signs. A fire door wedged open with the inverted sleeve of a child's coat. A pair of iron scissors stabbed into a wall-mounted hand sanitiser. The charms she placed to protect the innocent have been repurposed to deliver a stark message:

She's too late.

"Gremlins and fairies," she mutters, angrily. "Fairies and gremlins!" And then she scolds herself. It isn't the creatures' unprecedented collaboration that's beaten her; it's her own complacency. Many times she's felt the fangs of failure brush against her cheek but never in her thirteen years at the hospital have they managed to bite.

Until now.

Breathless, she arrives at the double doors of the maternity ward. Dangling from the door handle is another plastic jack-o'-lantern, grinning triumphantly. She unhooks it, drops it to the floor and crushes it under the heel of her boot. Then she throws open the doors, startling her scrubbed-up colleagues behind the reception desk. The room is alive with mothers changing nappies or wheeling their charges around on plastic trolleys. Nurses make routine checks and update their charts. Everything seems normal but it's not. The adults in the ward have a fog around their faces, a communal cataract that prevents them from seeing the truth of the monsters cradled in their arms. The oversized ears and pointed noses. The shrunken eyes and shrivelled wings. The withered bodies of ancient fairies suckling on the breasts of unsuspecting mothers.

For thirteen years she's kept the hospital free from mischief. She thought she was winning and genuinely believed she was in control, but she was wrong. They were here all along. Waiting. Working together. Complacency is the deadliest of sins and the cost of her failure is a roomful of parents whose babies have been stolen.

Switched.

Never to be returned.

LITTLE BLACK HOLES

They take our children first.

I'm walking Eddie home from school when we hear a horn sounding over and over. Up ahead I can see four of his classmates blocking the road. They just stand there, slack shouldered, staring at the shadows under the bus. The driver hits his horn again, shouting at them to get back on the pavement, but it's like they don't hear. Eddie wants to see what they're looking at but I pull him away, reminding him it's dangerous to play in the road.

Two days later, I find Eddie in his bedroom, enthralled by the darkness in the back of his wardrobe. I try to get his attention but he won't listen. I stand in front of him, blocking his view, and this noise erupts from his mouth that's relentless and urgent like a fire alarm. My skin prickles and I cover my ears, begging him to stop. He pushes me away and flees the room, bounding down the stairs towards the back garden. Through his bedroom window I see him staring into the hole under the shed, the one the foxes dug last winter. I run as fast as I can but, by the time I reach him, he's gone.

Not that it's easy to tell the difference. He still looks exactly like the sweet-natured boy in all the photos and his voice still sings to my heart. But he doesn't eat for pleasure anymore, only nutrition, and he's started downloading nonsense apps on his tablet that play nothing but TV static to the sound of twisting metal. If other parents are noticing the same things with their children, they don't say, but their eyes are puffed up like water wings so I know I'm not the only one who's worried.

I wake up in the middle of the night and Eddie's in my bedroom, staring out of the window. I ask him what he's doing and he tells me he's waiting. He won't say what for.

Over breakfast, we watch news reports of fathers being arrested for throwing their children out into the streets while grim-faced mothers linger in the background. The reporter says there's no evidence to suggest recent behavioural changes in minors are anything out of the ordinary. The official line is that we should remain calm and act responsibly.

Next they take the adults.

People post links to articles saying the safest time of day is after sunset. Discrete shadows are more dangerous than total darkness because the *signal*—that's what they call it—is more focused. Other news sites warn of an impending takeover, advising us to lock our children in their rooms and not take any chances. Pictures begin to surface of the military moving into major cities and there are rumours that when enough of the population has been converted there'll be a war. This all seems like scaremongering to me until I'm walking Eddie to school one morning and a tank stops to let us cross at the lights.

An actual tank, complete with caterpillar tracks and a cannon. Eddie holds my hand while we cross the road, both of us trying to act like everything's normal. But of course it isn't. I don't breathe again until the tank is out of sight.

Another night and Eddie's back in my room. I rest my hand on his shoulder and he looks at me, saying "Mummy? Where am I?" I sweep him up in my arms, desperately wanting to believe my little boy has returned to me, promising I won't let go this time. Then he asks me what I'm doing and I know it isn't him.

I think about quitting my job at the library but then I wonder what else would I do? I don't have a plan for this. All around me people continue to live their lives the way they've been taught to do since birth. The way they did as climate change reshaped the continents and plastic killed the oceans. The world is always ending but it's easier to carry on as if nothing is happening. So Eddie goes to school and I go to work, I'm just more careful about where I look. When I see someone standing motionless, staring into the darkness, I don't follow their gaze. Instead I bow my head, say a quick prayer and move on.

At home we watch YouTube tutorials on how to eliminate shadows by using blinds and mirrors to diffuse natural light. I feel guilty for not doing this sooner. Eddie whispers to his tablet while I replace our existing lightbulbs with lower watt, softer tone equivalents. Sometimes I wonder how much of him is still my son, and will he attack me in my sleep? And if he does, will I be able to fight back?

One evening we sit down to eat, Eddie and me, and I ask him if he's happy. When he doesn't reply, I look at him and notice he has tears in his eyes. I ask him what's wrong and he points to his left eye, saying it's probably just an eyelash. I offer to help and he leans towards me until I can practically taste the tomato soup on his breath. I pull his eyelids apart with my thumbs and tell him to look up, look down. There's nothing there. I tell him to look left but he looks right and we both laugh. Then I tell him to look straight at me and I fall into the deep and swirling blackness of his pupil.

WORRY DRAGONS

I need to switch the alarm clock off after five beeps but I'm all tangled up in my bedclothes and I don't get there until seven. Damn it. Those two extra beeps are like the first couple of rocks in a landslide. In this house, if things go wrong, people might die.

My suits are dry cleaned daily. I'd rather not think about the things that come into contact with my clothes but I can't help it. The disease-carrying insects that crawl where I'm not looking; the urine that trickles down the inside of my trouser leg after I've peed. Every surface has its own little microcosm of germs and parasites, just itching to relocate. After today's false start I dress myself with an extra dose of paranoia. Just because I'm not showing any signs of infection, doesn't mean I'm not ill— I might have asymptomatic bacteriuria or something equally insidious. My rule is if I can't pronounce it, I don't want it.

Ever since I was little, doctors have referred to my anxieties as 'worry dragons', as if giving them a cute name makes the slightest bit of difference.

When I leave the house, I go outside, close the door, open it again and stick my head back in to make sure everything is okay. On the way to work, I'm careful where

I tread, keeping my feet in the middle of the paving slabs and worrying that if I tread on a crack, I might fall through into the hot, sulphuric—

Oh shit.

I knew I'd forget something.

I run home as fast as I can, dancing like a man whose feet are on fire every time I step between two paving slabs. In the kitchen, I don't have time to hook an apron over my head or pull on a pair of shoulder-length veterinary gloves. Instead I dive into the chest fridge, lift out a twelve-pound slab of raw beef and a couple of racks of pork ribs with my bare hands and drop them in a bucket. And I know it's my imagination, but I'm sure I can feel Listeria monocytogenes crawling between my fingers and Escherichia coli nestling beneath my nails like little, tentacled tadpoles of death.

Just so you know, it's my fault everyone in my neighbourhood suffers with panic attacks and nightmares. And it's good they suffer because it means they're still alive.

I stop at the cellar door. I've done this many times before but this is the first time I've been late. Inside the cellar, the rotten-eggs smell of hydrogen sulphide brings tears to my eyes but I can't wipe them because my hands are still writhing with God knows what. Blinking furiously, I raise the bucket.

'Come on, girls,' I say.

Nothing.

'Come to Daddy.'

A slippery hiss. The rattling scales of an uncurling tail. My hands are shaking.

'I have food.'

And then they launch at me, one from each corner, eyes red, fangs exposed, roaring so ferociously it's like standing too close to the edge of the platform when a train rushes through.

Forget what my doctor says, these are my real worry dragons. And even though they're restrained, your average person would be in serious trouble at this point. I've seen salesman cry like babies and electricians reduced to quivering wrecks, just for being upstairs in my house. I even had to arrange a PO Box after a postman died on my doorstep. Close proximity to a worry dragon puts a huge amount of stress on the heart. Luckily for me, I'm used to dealing with a little extra anxiety.

Which isn't to say I'm safe. Or calm.

I try to tip the meat out of the bucket but it's jammed and won't come loose. Shaking it doesn't help. The dragons pace back and forth, tugging at their chains and snorting. They've been in captivity since birth but these days their restraints are little more than a gesture. Like toddlers who've grown too big for their cots, the truth is they could leave anytime they want. This is why I have to feed them promptly—because nobody wants a pair of hungry, full-grown worry dragons on the loose.

Smoke whispers from their nostrils. They bare their teeth and I can just make out their fire ducts, flickering with hungry flames. I'm so scared I can't imagine ever seeing daylight again, let alone taking my suits to the dry cleaners or telling my doctor to go fuck himself. As the dragons rise up on their hind legs, preparing to incinerate me, I can't imagine anything but my swift and agonising death in this cellar.

Two-handed, I swing the plastic bucket so it smashes against the wall. When it doesn't break I swing it again and again, trying to ignore the hisses and snorts behind me. On the fourth swing, the bucket splits and the raw, wet meat slaps against the concrete floor. As best I can, I toss it to the other side of the cellar.

While the dragons tear the meat to pieces, I hurry back upstairs, desperate to scrub my hands with bleach. I should have brought more food to apologise for being late. I shouldn't have been late. I'm amazed they didn't kill me.

In the hallway, I lean heavily against the reinforced, fire-resistant door until my breathing has slowed. Then I make my final mistake. Relaxing into the comforts of my usual routine, I open the door again and stick my head back inside to make sure everything is okay.

ANOTHER SIDE OF GUSTAV HOLST

Ralph stands in the valley beneath an allegro sky, watching sunset-pink clouds trilling in the breeze. The landscape is a masterpiece of desolation. Staccato stone pillars the size of industrial chimneys. Legato fissures like the claw marks of the Gods. He searches for familiar landmarks, anything beyond the elegy of rock and rubble, but finds nothing.

London is gone.

In the distance, he hears a screeching, screaming cacophony, reminiscent of violins complaining and trumpets straining against the warm, sulphuric air. He pictures giant, bird-like creatures, their wings beating and beaks stretched wide to reveal rows of razor teeth. A slow crescendo suggests the creatures are moving closer.

"What is this place?" he asks, breathless.

Clara's smile hints at a multitude of emotions. "This is Earth," she says.

***

The sitting room belonged to another decade. Antique frames on autumn-coloured wallpaper. A mahogany table and matching bureau. Candelabras and vases of dried flowers on the mantelpiece. Ralph squeaked into a leather-backed armchair and waited.

"Is this how it looked when Holst lived here?" he asked when Clara returned.

Clara ignored him. She might have been pretty in her youth but she'd long since acquired the hardened edges of someone accustomed to scorn. Her academic peers— mostly men—thought she lacked rigour and purpose. When she'd suggested that listeners couldn't fully appreciate the genius of The Planets suite without visiting the other planets, it confirmed their suspicions.

"I'm sorry," said Ralph. "My behaviour was inexcusable."

Two years ago, Clara was gifted the lease on Holst's former home in London, supposedly for research purposes. When Ralph learned of this, the strings of his patience were tuned so tightly something snapped. Why her? What had she done to deserve such special treatment? He was told that Clara had a fresh perspective. She had original ideas. Ralph was so upset, he devoted days of his time to discrediting her work, publishing his results to a chorus of approval from his colleagues.

Afterwards, he didn't hear from Clara for nearly eighteen months. Then she invited him to join her in London so she could personally present him with her latest discovery. Sitting in a polished leather armchair, in Holst's former home, Ralph felt mildly nauseous. It was one thing to riff for the entertainment of an academic crowd; it was another thing altogether to perform for a private audience.

"You might want to stand up for this," said Clara.

"Why am I here?"

"There are seven orchestral movements in The Planets suite. Every planet except Earth. Have you ever wondered why?"

Ralph scoffed. Then he remembered himself. "The movements represent the astrological characters," he replied. "Mars, the Bringer of War; Venus, the Bringer of Peace. There is no character for Earth."

Clara retrieved a manila folder from the bureau and passed it to him. Inside was a bundle of photocopied pages, bound with string. On the cover sheet, written in a familiar hand, were the words, "Bringer of Death."

***

The first dark shapes appear in the sky above the ridge, announcing their arrival with ugly, dissonant squawks. A perfect white crescent shimmers over the horizon, stark in its silence.

"It's magnificent, don't you think?" says Clara.

"How did we get here?"

"The music."

Ralph has no sense of scale. The flying creatures must be huge but they're tiny against the vast, cratered sphere rising behind them. It's so close he can see it moving. He can feel it in the gathering wind.

"Holst composed a doorway to another dimension," says Clara, her face alive with wonder. "And then he buried it behind a false wall in his cellar."

"Are we in danger?"

Below the squawking he can hear something else. A polyphonic swell of woodwind and timpani; the rush and splash of rolling cymbals.

"Holst was a coward," says Clara.

"Water," says Ralph. "I can hear water."

Beyond the horizon, the moon continues to rise.

***

In Clara's sitting room, Ralph read the crotchets and quavers like they were letters and words. In his head, he heard an overture of strings and cornets, music that teased in a style that was quintessentially Holst. But then, just as he'd grasped the mood of the piece, the clarinets rebelled. They fought against the melody, refusing to harmonise, pulling the major into minor before plunging into a shocking discord. The brass section panicked. The strings clung desperately to their martial rhythms but eventually they all succumbed to disorder.

"What is this?" he asked after he'd read the final, shocking cadence.

"Look up," said Clara.

The sitting room was gone. The bureau and the candelabras had vanished. Only Clara remained, and a landscape he didn't recognise.

***

"There are two Earths," says Clara. "Bringer of Life and Bringer of Death. Holst wrote movements for both. He created two doorways, one leading here, the other leading home."

"We can go back?" asks Ralph. "Where's the music?"

Clara taps a finger against the side of her head. "I've had Bringer of Life playing in here since we arrived."

As she speaks, Ralph notices she's becoming translucent. He grabs for her arm but his hand passes through empty air.

In a thin, reedy voice, Clara says, "Things could have been different between us."

"Take me with you. I'll tell everyone you were right."

But it's already too late. Like Neptune the Mystic, Clara has faded to nothing.

Ralph stands in the shadow of the moon as it drags the ocean crashing into the valley in front of him. The planet is exactly as Holst described it in his music. Above him, he hears the bass drum of beating wings. A crustacean the size of a tuba splatters across the ground where Clara was standing just moments ago. Dropped from the beak of God knows what.

He closes his eyes and tries to think. Saturn, the Bringer of Old Age; Jupiter the Bringer of Jollity. If he can just remember these movements, maybe he can find his way home to his own dimension.

But it's futile.

In his fear, his panic, he can't recall a single note.

THE LAMPPOST HUGGERS

It's six-thirty on a slush-wet Wednesday morning and I'm the only person at the bus stop who isn't nervous. The other commuters stare, mouths open, absent-mindedly scratching the backs of their wrists. On the far side of the road, an old man hugs a lamppost. In the orange light, his skin is sallow and wrinkled; his hair silver and flecked with snow. He's naked apart from a pair of threadbare pyjama shorts and when he moves his belly peels away from the frozen metal like Velcro.

It isn't just the old man who makes the other commuters nervous, it's what he represents. We've all seen the pictures in the news. We've heard the stories of ordinary people leaving their homes in the dead of night, with no clothes or shoes, searching for a lamppost to hug. They don't speak and won't let go without becoming hostile or suicidal. The best anyone can do is to keep them warm so they don't die from exposure. Yes, we've seen the photos, but that was London, Birmingham, Manchester. Not here. Not in our neighbourhood.

Not until this morning.

Two days later the old man is gone. In his place is a younger woman with a dressing gown tied loosely around her waist. There's something intimate about the way she hugs the lamppost, her ear pressed to its metal skin, a contented smile playing on her lips. Her husband is slumped on a nearby bench while her children tug on her dressing gown.

The woman isn't the only lamppost hugger on the high street this morning. Her family aren't the only ones mourning the loss of someone who's still alive. For as far as I can see in both directions, people of all ages cling to lampposts like lovers during a last dance.

The government has declared a state of national emergency but the huggers don't respond to curfews. Phrases like 'mass hysteria' and 'viral epidemic' have flown into the headlines and nested there. A video emerged of a priest in Rotherham persuading a lamppost-hugging member of his congregation to let go. For a day or so, the country dared to hope. Then the priest was photographed in red Paisley pyjamas, engaging in his own unorthodox embrace.

According to the leaflets, we're supposed to sleep with our clothes on. Not just clothes, but winter coats and boots. On the way home from work, I tell the bus driver this is no way to live. What's happening right now is a test of our national character and the only way to beat it is through strength of mind. That's why I still sleep in a T-shirt and shorts. That's why I'm still here and my neighbours are gone.

"I preferred it when the high street was lined with trees," says the bus driver as I step onto the icy pavement. "The birds did, too."

At home, I lie in bed and listen to the anguished howls of families begging their loved ones to come inside. I tell myself it won't be me. Not tonight. I repeat this over and over until it's imprinted on my subconscious.

I don't know what time it is when the high-pitched squeal tears me from my dreams. I clamp my hands over my ears and bury my head under the pillow, but the sound just gets louder, ringing like unchecked feedback from a guitar amp. Nauseous and disorientated, I fight my way out of bed and bump through the darkness, certain the noise must be coming from outside. On the way downstairs, I cling to the bannister and vomit on the carpet. Then I unlock the front door and fall face-first into the snow.

It isn't really me who grabs the lamppost. By the time I reach the far side of the road, I've lost the capacity for rational thought. The way a tortured man will confess to crimes he didn't commit, I'm willing to try anything. The moment my skin touches the metal, the noise changes, the lamppost acting like some kind of antenna. Gone is the screaming static. Instead, my head is filled with the soothing music of angels. Beautiful overlapping melodies. Notes as delicate as the falling snow.

This must be what heaven sounds like.

Then I hear another noise above me. A low, soft whoomph. I look up into the darkness, waiting and wondering. The smell arrives first, ripe and sticky like the local dump. Then the creature lands on the arm of the lamppost, each wing as wide as a bus. Its toes are mattress springs and vacuum cleaner hoses, curled into lawnmower-blade talons. Its feathers are shredded pillow cases and ironing-board covers. The way it jerks and twitches, it reminds me of birds on a feeder. But there aren't any birds this big. And this one has three heads, massive like chimineas, with dangerously-hooked beaks.

The creature is the source of the song I can hear. I don't care if it's an angel calling me to heaven or a siren luring me to my death; I'm ready either way. The middle head stops singing and twists to one side, inspecting me with a black webcam eye. I reach up and it lunges towards me, hissing and spitting, its beak stretched impossibly wide. One snap of those fearsome jaws and my head would come clean off. And maybe I should be afraid but I'm not. I'm its servant, its disciple, and as long as it sings to me it may do whatever it desires. But something else snatches its attention.

The night bus, growling like a beast up the high street.

The middle head twists towards the others, hissing instructions, and with a flap of its wings, the creature disappears over the rooftops. I panic and start to follow, but the moment I let go of the lamppost, the noise returns.

I'm winded by the cold. I fall back and press my ear to the soothing metal.

It's okay. I can still hear its song.

TWO WEEKS TO WOLF

You want to know what I think it was? Sure you do. That's why you came out here, right? You want me to tell you it was a coyote-wolf hybrid so you can go back to sleeping at night. Let me ask you a question first. How long have you been driving? Three years? So the Great Falls Tribune sent a rookie. Good for you, kid. Have a seat and I'll tell you everything I know.

Have you been out to Alma's ranch, yet? It's right on the edge of Flinton, overlooking acres of nothin'. Just ranch and shrubland all the way to the horizon. It's easy to get spooked in a place like that. Alma was on her ranch when she shot the creature, right around dusk. It ain't illegal to shoot a wolf as long as you report it, which she did. The problem is it wasn't a wolf. You've seen the photos, right? Oversized paws and ears, canines a little longer than you might expect—like a drawing of a wolf by someone who ain't ever seen a real one. Jim Shelton, from the Department of Parks and Wildlife, drove it out to the forensics lab at Oakland for DNA testing. He reckoned it'd be two weeks before they announced the results.

It turns out that two weeks is a long time in Flinton, Montana.

In the days that followed, I heard it was a dire wolf, a dog man and a Chupacabra. Then Mike Riddick from the Post Office said maybe Alma shot herself a werewolf. Now I don't believe in werewolves any more than you do, but people let their imaginations run wild when they're bored and ill-informed. And once Alma was sure there ain't no law against shooting mythical beasts, she went right along for the ride. Did you see her on TV talking about silver bullets?

She quieted down real quick when it turned out Lucy Berger was missing.

Lucy was always a wilful child, with a history of running away whenever the mood took her, so no one thought much of her disappearance until Alma shot her wolf. Then folks started speculatin' and drew some interesting conclusions. Lucy's pug-nose and monobrow probably didn't help matters. The thing is, to become a werewolf, you need to be scratched by one—and no one could remember Lucy being scratched.

Reverend Johnson, the black preacher over at United Methodist, said he had a theory. Lucy's father, who used to go hunting before Lucy was born, was up in Highwood Mountains one year when he disturbed a bear. It clawed him real bad on his leg and folks said he was lucky to make it down from the mountain alive. A couple of inches higher and Lucy might never have been conceived. After Alma shot her wolf, Reverend Johnson asked his congregation to cast their minds back. Were they sure it was a bear that clawed Lucy's father? Or could it have been somethin' … less natural?

Could Lucy have inherited her affliction?

Last Friday, after the Berger family had packed up and left town to avoid all the unwanted attention, Sheriff Hayes drove out to the Department of Parks and Wildlife to speak to Jim Shelton. The sheriff has a big appetite and a bone-dry sense of humour, and she knows Flinton better than anyone. She could see there was trouble brewin' and wanted to head it off before things got out of hand. She asked Jim to go on record saying werewolves don't exist and Jim suggested she visit Oakland to see for herself.

At the Oakland lab, they escorted the sheriff down to the sub-basement to show her the creature's body. Only, when they pulled the drawer out, it wasn't a wolf anymore. It was little Lucy Berger with a bullet hole the size of a sunflower blossoming on her chest.

I'm messin' with you! You should see your face.

They had the creature all stretched out on a table so the sheriff could see its empty eyes, oversized cuspids, and cocoa fur all stiff with blood. The test results weren't back so Sheriff Hayes took more photos—ones you won't find in the newspapers—and brought them to me because she knew I used to breed hybrids back in the day. She was sittin' right where you are when she heard United Methodist was on fire.

We don't have a lot of black folks in Flinton and I think it's fair to say a small percentage of the population objected to Reverend Johnson spreading rumours about white folks being werewolves. When the fire department found evidence of arson, Johnson started preaching in the streets and black folks arrived by the busload from Lewistown and Big Sandy to support him. The protest started out peaceful enough, as they often do, but then it turned ugly and Mike's Post Office went up in flames.

Flinton, with a population just shy of four hundred, became a war zone. Black folks were angry because some white folks had burned down their church. White folks were upset because their town was full of angry blacks. And ranchers were worried about werewolves killing their livestock.

Sheriff Hayes was done messin' around. She called the governor and asked him to send in the National Guard.

And all because of a dead canine.

Before she left, I told the sheriff appearances can be deceiving. Sure, it looks like a coyote-wolf hybrid in the photos but I think there's more to it than that.

The DNA results are due back any day but even they won't tell you the whole story, kid. They won't tell you the creature was cursed or that our town is tearin' itself to pieces because Alma killed it. If you really wanna know what that creature was when it was alive, you need understand the mark it's made in death. Only then will you have your answer.

FLEDGLINGS

There's a girl next door who puts dead flies in her sandwiches. She catches them on curls of flypaper, which she hangs from her porch, and uses tweezers to remove their bodies once they've stopped twitching. Most times they leave their legs behind but not always. On a typical day she'll catch around twenty but last week I heard her count to thirty-six. She transfers the flies to a slice of rye bread, squishing their bodies into glossy lashings of butter. When she's finished, she folds the bread in half and places it in her lunchbox next to a bruised banana and a slice of malt loaf.

At school, my friends' eyes grow wide when I tell them. Then they shake their heads.

"We need to see for ourselves," says Owen.

I try to reply but my mouth gets stuck on the first consonant and I end up popping like a goldfish.

"We need proof, Stutter-man" says George.

The following morning, Owen and George call for me before school. My mum's still in her nightie and I'm halfway through a bowl of Sugar Puffs. I stop eating to show my friends up to my bedroom.

They gasp when the girl appears on her porch, tweezers in hand. Owen wants to confront her, but I grab his arm and shake my head.

"After school," I say. "While my m-m-mum's in w-work."

Later, we form a wall in front of my neighbour's house and watch the girl as she arrives home. I stand at the end nearest my house, wishing I'd never told anyone. The girl slows down when she sees us.

"Are you the girl who eats dead flies?" asks Owen.

The girl shrugs.

"We saw you put them in a sandwich."

The girl thinks about it. Then she nods.

"Why?"

"Come inside and I'll show you."

We follow her into a dark hallway that smells of earthworms and leaf mulch. The walls and floor are covered in scraps of plastic, fabric, string, bark and dried leaves. Underneath a lampshade, I can see the jagged glass of a broken lightbulb.

We shouldn't be here. I want to apologise and leave. The girl closes the door before I can find the words.

"Step on through," she says, gesturing towards the kitchen.

The walls of the kitchen are lined with cupboards, a sink, a fridge and an oven. Like the hallway, the floor is a mess of twigs and straw and other soft materials. In the centre of the room is a large, rectangular dining table with six chairs. The table has long scratches in its wooden surface and a giant, porcelain fruit bowl in the middle.

"Meet my parents," says the girl.

I look around, confused, and then I spot them perched on top of the wall units. Like gargoyles. Their bodies look almost human—him in a lumberjack shirt and jeans, her in a sweatshirt and jogging bottoms—but for tufts of dark feathers around their wrists and ankles. Instead of feet, they have long, banded toes ending in claws. And their heads—those terrible, feathered heads—have gunmetal beaks and enormous black eyes. I turn to run but only make it as far as the hall before something hits me from behind.

Darkness follows.

I wake up to the sound of screaming, followed by a wet, gargled plea. My chest feels heavy and my arms won't move. I open my eyes and there is blood everywhere.

I pull hard against the thick coil of rope that binds me to the kitchen chair, but it's useless. Owen is tied up next to me. On the other side of Owen, George's eyes have been gouged out and tears of blood pour down his cheeks. His mouth is open and I'm pretty sure his tongue has been torn off. His neck has been ripped to ribbons. I look away in disgust.

"Don't scream," says the girl, sitting opposite us. "They don't like it."

Next to me, Owen mumbles. He's shivering and he smells of urine.

"You need to sing" says the girl. "Like this." She opens her mouth and a tune comes out, wordless and without joy, but enough for me to recognise Greensleeves. One of the bird creatures hops up onto the table, its claws digging fresh grooves in the surface. And then I notice that the fruit bowl is full of mealworms, ribbed and writhing in their own faeces, each one several inches long and as fat as a sausage. The bird creature pecks one in half with its beak and leans towards the girl who opens her mouth wide. The still-wriggling worm is passed from parent to child, who accepts it dutifully. I feel sick. I fight the urge to scream.

"It's your turn now," says the girl. "Sing."

Owen shakes his head and screws up his face. "I'm not singing. Not for that."

The other bird creature hops up onto the table and the two of them look down on Owen, heads twitching, their eyes fierce and expectant.

"No," says Owen, sliding backwards.

I want to plead with him but the words are jagged rocks that get stuck in my throat.

Sunlight catches the sharp edge of a beak as the first bird creature stabs downwards. Owen chokes in surprise as they peck at his face and neck, and I turn my face away to avoid being sprayed with his blood.

Opposite me, the girl is still chewing. "How about you?" she says. "Will you sing?"

One of the bird creatures plucks another worm from the bowl, ready to feed it to me.

I tell myself I can do this. I know songs. I'm in the school choir. And I don't even need the words; it's enough to sing the tune.

But I can feel my stutter waiting for me.

It wants me to fail.

WEATHER CYCLE

Leanne watches footage of climate protesters glued to government buildings, and wonders if her ex-partner, Jess, is among them. Against a backdrop of swirling smoke and forest fires, the weather reporter says it's officially the hottest spring on record. Outside, Leanne's porch light is always on and the wheelie bin vomits cardboard from its mouth. Three recycling boxes, never used, are stacked neatly by the shed.

At three o'clock, she tells her boss she'll call back later. She needs to put a wash on before she fetches her daughter, Isla, from school. The new washer-dryer arrived that morning, with a giant 'Environmentally Unfriendly' sticker on the side of the box—a bargain thanks to government deregulation.

She shoves Isla's football kit into the drum and selects a super-hot, super-quick cycle, smiling because she knows Jess wouldn't approve. When she presses 'Start', she's blinded by a flash of light.

Lightning? But there isn't a cloud in the sky.

She's halfway up the road when it hits her from behind with enough force to knock her to the ground. Except the ground isn't there anymore. The noise is loud, like a thousand breaking bottles. The colour is mud with sporadic patches of snow-white foam. The smell is soap suds and shower drains. And it's steaming. She's thrown against the window of a parked car, her shoulder exploding with pain. She claws at the slippery surface and manages to hold on to one of the roof rails until the surge has passed. Her arm throbs and her clothes are soaked through. The whole street is flooded, with water pressing against front doors and reaching up for ground-floor windows. She wants to save her house, but what can she do?

And Isla might be in danger.

The floodwater is nearly to her waist as Leanne wades towards the school. A pushchair floats past and she lunges for it, wanting to make sure it's empty, but a wheelie bin smashes into her ribs and sends her tumbling backwards. By the time she's back on her feet, the pushchair is gone.

Nothing makes sense. She doesn't live on a flood plain. Could a tsunami have reached this far inland?

Before she can finish this thought, a thousand tiny explosions shatter the surface of the water. She spins around, searching for the source, and sees people crying and covering their heads. Then it hits her: hard, sharp and cold.

The clear blue skies have been replaced by roiling clouds that grumble overhead. It's raining so hard, Leanne fears she's going to drown standing up. And then something grabs her arm, pulling her sideways under the shelter of a shop's awning.

"It's just a cloudburst," says a voice—concerned, male. "It'll pass."

Leanne clings to him while she catches her breath. "I have to fetch my daughter," she says. More people join them under the awning and they stay that way until the rain eases off.

Isla.

Leanne lurches back down the road in the direction of the school, trying not to imagine the children trapped behind classroom doors, crying as they fight for space on the tables, floating face down in deserted corridors. She pushes through an island of plastic bottles and food trays, a town's worth of recycling forming an unnatural barrier. And there it is: Isla's school. She smiles with relief when she sees the wall of children standing behind their classroom windows, safe and waving, their noses squished against the glass.

As she enters the playground, something ruffles her hair and bites her cheeks. The other parents feel it to. They hesitate, alarmed, but they can't see what Leanne can see because they're too close to the building. And she envies them that.

Behind the school, rising like an umbilical cord to the clouds, is a dark, black tornado. Leanne's never seen anything like it. She knows she should do something but she can't think. She can't move. Someone shouts "Run!" and she joins the other parents as they hurry forward, funnelling up the ramp and in through the main school doors. When she arrives at Isla's classroom, she tells the children to get away from the windows before leading them to the assembly hall. She's barely aware she's holding Isla's hand until they stop. Then she lifts her daughter in her arms and sobs against her shoulder while the building rattles around them.

An hour later, they walk home through a world filled with unimaginable destruction. The water has mostly dispersed, but the streets are cluttered with felled trees, upturned cars and sections of dislodged roof. Garden swings and trampolines lie crushed and broken, their metal frames sparkling in the sunshine. Leanne shields Isla from the sight of a body bag being loaded into the back of an ambulance, and notices the pushchair hanging from the arm of a lamppost. She still can't see if it's empty.

The sun presses against their backs, making the air thick and sweet with the scent of lavender. Leanne's clothes are sticky and she can feel her scalp turning red. But Isla's at her side and she's too tired to care about anything else.

They arrive home just as the new washer-dryer completes its cycle. Leanne's impressed. While the world around them went to hell, her new appliance did the job she bought it to do. She stops when she notices the words printed in grey around the dial:

Soak. Rinse. Spin. Dry.

Flood. Rain. Tornado. Sun.

The tremor starts at her feet and rises quickly to her chest. She fears it's the result of an earthquake or another tornado, but it's not. It's her nerves. She's exhausted.

"There's someone at the door," calls Isla.

Leanne splashes down the hall to see who it is. Outside, a lorry casts a shadow across the front of the house. A man in overalls wheels a large box up the drive.

A new chest freezer.

Another bargain.

Another box with 'Environmentally Unfriendly' on the side.

Leanne claps her hands together in delight and asks him to bring it to the kitchen door at the side of the house.

PART THREE

"Death is only a translation of life into another language."

–F. Marion Crawford

SUMMER SNOW

She knows there's no such thing as snow in summer. Not here in rural France, where the sun beats down over acres of pasture, hot enough to crack the earth. She blinks her powder-blue eyes, her eyelashes so fine they're nearly invisible, and looks again. The snow is still there, too uniform to be flower petals or some environmental pollutant. She touches a withered fingertip to the bedroom window, half-expecting to feel the bitter kiss of winter—but the glass is cool, not cold. If only Rob were with her. He always knew how to put her at ease.

The following morning, her curiosity rouses her with the cockerel. On the far side of the road, beyond the ancient oak and horse chestnuts, the field is white from one corner to the next. A solitary pony flaps its tail and nuzzles the snow, its teeth snagging the grass underneath. She wonders if this is what the government meant when they declared a 'climate emergency'. Not islands consumed by the sea or villages flattened by the wind, but more-localised anomalies.

Rob, her husband, had died the previous winter, not far from their home in the Lake District. She can't remember if it was the fall that killed him or the cold. Such details are of no interest to her if they can't bring him back.

As the hot French sun bakes the afternoon, flies dart through the cottage, buzzing against windows and disrupting the peace. She'd swat them if she wasn't so preoccupied. Why wasn't the snow thawing? Surely it should have turned to water by now. Instead, it's halfway across the road.

Enough.

Outside, the heat's unbearable, even under her floppy hat. The air is alive with the scent of summer blossom and the chirp of insects. She unlocks the shed next to the log store and retrieves a shovel before marching to the middle of the road. The pony lifts its head and watches her warily.

At her feet, the snow sparkles and shifts as though a small mammal is moving underneath it. "Why haven't you melted?" she asks. She lowers the spade to scrape the snow back to the verge and, as she does so, the snow rushes towards her in a low and urgent wave. The sudden cold shocks her sandaled feet and ankles. Another wave approaches, this time resembling many giant arms, all of them reaching for her. The spade clatters against the tarmac as she hurries back to the safety of her cottage.

That night, she lies in bed and tries to remember what it was like to have Rob lying next to her. His cool body that always welcomed her touch. The minty smell of toothpaste on his breath. His sleepy grumble that was never quite a snore. She remembers the late-night ring of the doorbell and the grave-looking policewoman standing on her porch. She shook her head violently when the policewoman explained what had happened. It couldn't be true. Rob had promised to come home to her and he always kept his promises.

At first light, she wraps her dressing gown around her shoulders and hurries to the window, brushing away the bodies of dead flies lying on the sill. She stares through the glass, dumbfounded. Every inch of the landscape, from her front door to the horizon, is perfectly white.

Fearing witchcraft or the devil's work, she hurries downstairs to find her mobile phone, which has half a battery and a single bar of signal. She calls her daughter's number and it rings without going to voicemail. Her son's phone doesn't even connect. She rummages through the cottage's 'Welcome' folder until she finds the contact details for the emergency services. Then she wonders what she'll say. And whether they'll speak English. When the low battery warning pops up on the screen, she decides to check outside again before she makes another call.

She pulls back the blind and gasps. Maybe it's the just the shadows of tree branches swaying in the sun, but it looks as though the snow outside is moving—rolling and tumbling like a turbulent sea. She jumps backwards as a frozen wave hammers against the front door, forcing a thin line of snow underneath and onto her welcome mat.

It's found a way in.

She takes the phone upstairs and tries to call her children again but there's still no answer. She stares out of the window, paces the room, and checks her phone, feeling like a prisoner in her own home. As the day wears on, she slips under her duvet and lies there, examining every muffled thump. She's convinced the snow is spreading through the cottage; waves pushing it forwards, arms pulling it up.

If only Rob were here with her. She remembers the blizzard, the policewoman saying he'd slipped on the ice. Was it the fall that killed him, or the cold? By the time the policewoman told her, she'd stopped listening.

When she wakes up, the room is darker, cooler. She rolls over to face the bedroom door and recoils in shock. The floor is white where it used to be grey. She pulls the duvet around her shoulders, trying to think, trying desperately not to panic. All around her, the snow rises and falls as though it's breathing. She crawls to the edge of the bed and peers over, fingers clinging to the mattress, eyes wide with fear. There's a familiar smell—minty, like toothpaste.

"Rob?" she asks.

The snow parts, creating a safe path from the bed to the bedroom door.

She's free to leave.

Of course she is.

As she watches, the snow forms into a hand, which reaches towards her.

"Rob," she says again, stepping into the snow.

The snow wraps an ice-cold arm around her, holding her firm in its frozen embrace.

And finally she remembers.

It wasn't the fall that killed her husband.

ENDANGERED

Once the mist has cleared, Tommy and I make our way through the sweet wreaths of heather to observe what's left of the gentoo penguin colony. Their population, like ours, has been decimated by the rapidly changing environment. I doubt they'll last another season.

Crouching low, Tommy sweeps his fringe aside and studies the penguins through his binoculars. "Clarence, Wingtip…" I've asked him not to name them but he's wilful like his mum. Every time he spots a distinctive feature, a name is quick to follow.

In the eight years since he was born, the world has changed beyond recognition. Nations have been fragmented or lost altogether. The North Pole is underwater and so is our hometown in Dorset. I transferred to the Falklands when Tommy was three, with a grant to study the impact of climate change on the local birdlife. The money's gone but we linger on like shadows waiting for one last sunset.

"Oyster, Flag…" With his spare hand, Tommy rubs the dulled silver of his mum's crucifix pendant, which he's worn around his neck since she passed away. He says he doesn't miss her but the crucifix tells a different story.

In the last few years we've watched the penguins retreat towards the cliffs as their beach has been reclaimed by the sea. We've seen disease and famine decimate their ranks. I've explained to Tommy that their world is ending and so is ours, but still he wakes up every morning with a smile that's ripe with hope. I want him to count the days of our continuing existence but instead he counts the penguins, reciting "Flappy, Duckface, Hood," until I tell him to stop.

"I can't find Grizzly," he says, alarmed. I'm about to help him search for the old-timer when we spot the birds of prey circling near the clifftop. Below them, a penguin chick has ventured beyond the edge of the colony.

"What are they, Daddy?"

I check through my binoculars and count five striated caracaras, what the locals call Johnny rooks. The first caracara drops out of the sky followed by the others until the penguin chick is surrounded. Tommy wants to intervene but I hold him back, reminding him the caracaras have chicks to feed too.

He looks away, clutching his crucifix and praying for the penguin's life. I've never seen him pray before and he offers such a passionate plea to heaven, he reminds me of his mum.

"Do you pray often?"

"At night I pray for you and Mummy and if I'm still awake I pray for me, too."

I tousle his hair, remembering how lucky I am to be alive.

"Will God save us?" asks Tommy.

I think about how best to respond before nodding. "I'm sure he will."

Satisfied, Tommy returns to his binoculars. Seconds later he spots Grizzly and squeals with delight. He's probably thinking if Grizzly can make it, so can we. And I really want to believe him.

At the bottom of the cliffs, the caracaras tear and gouge.

AND THE WORLD
ROARED BACK

They hear it long before they see it. In the playground, the two boys grip the cold bars of the climbing frame until their hands hurt. The bomber appears high above their heads, dinosaur big and just as ugly, tearing the clouds asunder. Wide eyed, they watch as it roars across a sprawling blanket of rooftops before disappearing into the horizon.

"I wish I had a jet plane," says Sam dropping back down to a crouch and flattening the rolling paper against his jeans. "Because that's how fast I'd be out of here." His life is a misery-go-round of unsolicited opinions, unfinished homework and unfathomable feelings towards girls. "Mum's become a monster nag," he says, flicking the hair out of his face. "All she ever does is moan and wish I were dead."

"If lions roared like that," says Ollie, still staring at the sky, "shit, if anything else roared like that, we wouldn't be top of the food chain."

In the aftermath of so much noise, they barely register the distant sirens. The playground, with its squeaky swings and sticky slides, has been their safe place since they started school a decade ago. Nothing can hurt them in their climbing frame fortress.

"Sam," says Ollie, "hide."

Sam's mum appears, barefoot and out of breath. She seems incomplete, like a drunk without a drink. "Where's Sam?" she asks. "I thought he was with you."

Ollie shrugs.

"Damn it, Ollie, where is he?"

"I haven't seen him, Mrs Boston."

"You have to go home. Your parents will be looking for you. And if you see Sam, for God's sake tell him to find me."

Ollie waits until she's left the park and then taps twice on the metal tube connecting the two halves of the climbing frame. Sam emerges triumphantly, holding a crisply rolled cigarette between his finger and thumb like it's the key to adulthood.

"Not bad for a first try," says Ollie, taking the cigarette. "What's up with your mum?"

"She's probably been nosing around in my bedroom again."

Sam pats his pockets for his lighter but gets distracted by movement on the far side of the park. A black hatchback squeezes through the gates of the main entrance and bumps across the uneven playing field, its wheels ripping up the grass as it races towards the side gate. It's nearly there when it hits a tree root and bounces out of control, crunching into the stone perimeter wall. The boys hear the driver cursing as he slams his car door.

"What's going on?" asks Sam. All around the park, the traffic is stationary in both directions. Even the blue-flashing ambulance is stuck. He's never seen anything like it. And the park is empty. There are no joggers or dog-walkers doing laps of the field, no smokers in leather jackets hanging out by the toilets and no kids baiting their parents in the playground. "Where did everyone go?"

"The park belongs to us now," says Ollie, putting the cigarette to his lips.

Sam finds the lighter in his back pocket and holds it up, trembling in anticipation. This is what independence feels like. This, right now, is all the future that matters. "I never want to turn into my parents," he says.

"Give me a light," says Ollie.

Sam rolls the spark wheel and the world around him flickers like lightning. He blinks away the blindness, thinking he's somehow responsible. In the silence that follows, a warm draught steals the flame from his lighter. It reminds him of his last holiday with his parents and the moment they stepped off the air-conditioned plane into the hot Spanish sun. But then he has to close his eyes against an onslaught of grit and dust. Someone calls his name. Squinting, he turns towards the voice and sees a small figure running through the park, reaching towards him.

"Mum?"

Behind her, a giant shadow rises up from the horizon, pressing against the clouds like an enchanted beanstalk with branches of smoke and fire. Beneath it, a ripple spreads through the rooftops. All around the park, windows shatter and alarms ring out. People abandon their cars and run.

Sam drops the lighter and it pings off the climbing frame to the soft floor of the playground below. His mum is halfway towards him but the field is melting behind her. Flames flash across the grass the way the sea rushes up the shore. She's moving fast but nowhere near fast enough.

Sam cries out to her, urging her to hurry.

The world roars back.

LEPIDOPTERA

Right now, in this interrogation room, I feel like I'm in someone else's body. My muscles and bones don't seem to fit and I have to make a conscious effort to satisfy basic urges, like blinking and breathing. The arresting officer, Jenkins, massages the bags under his eyes. He's rattled and I wonder what he saw. How bad it was. He slurps coffee from one of those novelty mugs where the clothes disappear when you add hot water and tells me again how much he hates being stuck in here with me. "Your kid sister," he says. "For Christ's sake, she was only eleven." My sister, Jess, is dead and he's annoyed because I haven't confessed yet.

It was the third night in a row I'd gone to the cinema to watch the horror double bill and the whole thing was beginning to feel like a recurring nightmare. My dad had been giving me a hard time since I lost my job at the pizza restaurant and I couldn't bear the sight of him and Jess all curled up on the sofa, Jess snuggling into the crook of his arm the way I used to when I was her age. It was horrible. I had to get out.

I never expected to meet anyone at the cinema but there she was: Natalya, with the pearlescent skin and east-European accent. I watched how she fluttered from one shadow to the next, not realising that she'd already settled on the chair next to mine. Later she said she was drawn to me because she saw darkness in my soul. She asked questions about my family and I probably should have been suspicious, but I've always found it difficult to think straight around pretty girls. As the clock hands fell from the midnight hour, we left the cinema and she followed me home.

The police dragged me from my house around 4am following an anonymous tip-off. Jenkins said I was half-crazed, like an animal in a trap, clawing and biting at anyone who came near. It took three officers to put me in cuffs and two more to get me into the patrol car. He said I threw up when I saw the flashing blue lights.

"Does any of this sound familiar?" he asks in the interrogation room. It does, but only because he's told me this story about half a dozen times already. "What about the painting on the wall?" he asks. "Whose blood was it?"

I don't know anything about a painting. The last thing I remember, Natalya was on top of me, the bedsheet spread between her outstretched arms like a pair of wings. She leaned towards me, leaving crimson kisses on my chest and neck, and asked if I wanted to be free. I closed my eyes and felt like I was flying.

"And what was it supposed to be?" asks Jenkins. "Some sort of butterfly?"

I don't know about butterflies either. I couldn't tell you the different types or what they eat or how long they live.

The only thing I know for sure about butterflies is something my dad used to say: they start out earthbound and then God gives them wings.

Jenkins wants to know if the painting is a gang sign or cult symbol. I shrug and he thinks I'm being cute. "You didn't see it?" he asks. "Let me show you." He hands me a photo of the crime scene. My dad's on the bed, grey-skinned and awkwardly-posed, his eyes staring blankly at the ceiling. Jess is slumped over him. And I know I should feel something but I don't.

On the wall above them is a painting about the size of a grown man's shadow. Crimson palm prints and little finger lines. The creature on the wall has two antenna; ruler-straight and perpendicular. They're joined by a third, diagonal line connecting the tip of the left hand antenna to the root of the right. It looks like sloppy handwork, but it isn't. It's an "N".

Natalya.

And it isn't a butterfly. Butterflies are daytime creatures, feeding and basking in the sun. The painting on my dad's bedroom wall is a moth, a creature of the night, and finally I understand. I was supposed to be caught. Being arrested is part of my induction into a new way of life. Natalya has given me wings, now I need to learn how to fly.

"Your father and sister were exsanguinated," says Jenkins, slurping his coffee from his naked woman mug. "What happened to the rest of their blood?"

How should I know? Maybe Natalya took it. Maybe she drank it. The thought of their warm blood on her lips is strangely appealing.

Something stirs inside me. An acceptance of who I've become. Of the monster Natalya created. I lean closer to Jenkins, close enough to see the veins throbbing in his wrists, and utter my first words since I was arrested.

"I want to paint a picture with you."

UNDER A BLACK GLASS CEILING

Jade remembers how excited she felt when she saw the advert promising the culinary delights of a long-forgotten culture. She switched off her phone so she could listen, without distraction, to the radio interview with the man who may or may not have been the seven-years-missing, Michelin-starred chef. "I don't want my new restaurant to be exclusive," he'd said. "The super-rich are only interested in bragging to their friends, and food critics will spoil the mystery for future diners. We pride ourselves on the diversity of our menu, which is why we value diversity in our clients."

How could she resist?

The restaurant, situated in an industrial hub outside the city, is hard to miss. Even in darkness, the architecture is eccentric. The entrance is guarded by statues of lion-headed men with barrel chests and serpentine tales, their faces fixed in hungry roars. Dozens of carved-stone hands reach out from the window frames as though previous diners were frozen while trying to claw their way free. The domed roof bulges like a squashed water balloon, glowing green and silver against the night sky. Most impressive of all is the spire on top of the dome, a needle of black granite that reaches up beyond the clouds.

At eight o'clock, the queue goes quiet when the maître-d' opens the doors.

Jade shoves her hands into her jacket pockets to keep them from shaking. She's tired of her restaurant reviews being published in hidden corners of local newspapers. Of the constant struggle to be noticed and the sense she'll never be good enough. She longs to be a household name and tonight is her big opportunity. After the tickets for entry were drawn at random from an online lottery, she emptied her savings account and bought one through a black-market website. She's desperate for the scoop of a lifetime, a story no one else can tell.

Inside, the restaurant is disappointingly mundane.

A waiter, wearing a black waistcoat over a midnight blue shirt, provides Jade with a complimentary glass of Champagne before escorting her to her table. He places a wicker basket of freshly-baked rolls by her elbow, the bread crusted with whole grains and smelling faintly of anchovies. She asks questions but the waiter gives nothing away, other than to promise a "once-in-a-lifetime experience" for everyone.

The only striking feature of the restaurant's interior is the ceiling: a solid sheet of black material, maybe acrylic, which has been polished into a mirror. Jade leans back in her chair and walks her eyes across the reflected room, seeing ghostly fingers fiddling with cutlery, lips kissing

Champagne flutes, and heads bobbing to the tune of a hundred hungry stomachs. But something is wrong. Where have the waiters gone? And where's the aroma of freshly-cooked food?

Opening-night jitters, no doubt. She's seen it often enough.

Her eyes are drawn back to the ceiling and she realises that, behind every reflection, the darkness has depth. The material is no longer opaque; it's some sort of glass. In every shadow, she can see the white pinpricks of distant stars. Galaxies spiralling across the night sky. Great mysteries unwinding to infinity. Her instincts tell her to record everything, every thought and whisper, and she fights the urge to reach for the notebook she keeps in her handbag.

A bell rings, loud and crisp. "Ladies and gentlemen," says the maître-d'. "Thank you for joining us on this most … triumphant of occasions. I trust you enjoyed your Champagne. I hope you enjoyed the bread. Now it's time for the main course."

The lights go out and a scream erupts from the far side of the room. Glasses crash against empty plates and chairs scrape the carpet as diners flee their tables. In darkness, it's possible to see clearly through the ceiling, to witness the vast cosmos in all its radiant beauty. But there's something moving up there, something so big it would cast the whole city in shadow. Jade stares in horror as the snout of what looks like a giant reptile floats above them, with armoured skin covered in luminescent scales, and teeth that must be ten times the size of elephant tusks. The creature rolls on its side, revealing a single eye with a long, narrow pupil and an iris that burns red and gold. It watches, unblinking, as panic unfolds in the restaurant.

Crowds gather around the exits, tugging on handles, ramming the doors with shoulders, but it's futile. A chair flies towards a window and bounces uselessly to the floor. With creeping dread, Jade realises they're trapped.

Like lobsters in a tank.

The creature slips a long, scaly appendage through the black-glass ceiling, which ripples like the surface of a pond. Jade's eyes sting as the air is filled with the stench of rotting fish. She wipes away her tears in time to see the creature pluck a young man from the restaurant floor and lift him up to its mouth, shoving him in whole. The man's legs flail briefly before being crunched between the creature's mighty jaws. The other diners scream and huddle in corners until the creature swipes at them, sending them scurrying across the floor.

A middle-aged businesswoman is next to go.

Then a father trying to protect his children.

Through it all, Jade remains seated. She feels oddly relieved. No one is leaving the restaurant; their fates have already been determined. And yet the story isn't over. Editors have rejected her opinions about chefs and restaurants and opening night misadventures, but she's sure they'll want to hear this one—even if she won't be around to tell it.

She used to tell the story; now she is the story.

The food critic who became the main course.

Feeling a surge of inspiration, she removes a notebook and pen from her handbag. If she's quick, she might be able to scribble some last words.

BOÎTE FANTÔME

I pretend to be grieving because that's what people do at funerals, right? They knuckle fake tears from their eyes while secretly checking their watches to see if it's time to go. A magpie cackles from the roof of the crematorium and I'm surrounded by a half circle of sombre-faced mourners offering condolences, hugs and tissues. I think the passing of my mother-in-law should be a cause for celebration. Never again will she put the cutlery back in the wrong trays or forget to refill the water jug after she's used it to top up the kettle.

I can't say I'll miss her.

On the other side of the carpark, my wife talks to a man I don't recognise. He's a little taller than her, with greying hair and a look that says, 'If I concentrate hard enough, I might live forever.' It's a look I've seen before in the vineyards and auberges of rural France. My mother-in-law spent her teenage years in Provence so maybe he's an old friend. He pulls a box the size of a human skull out of nowhere and holds it up for my wife to see. When she touches it, the magpie flies from the crematorium roof.

Two weeks later, our savings account is empty. Ignoring the speed limit on the way home, I phone the bank and navigate the automated queues until I arrive at the hold music. "All our operators are busy at the moment," says the pre-recorded voice. I pull onto our drive and nearly hit the Frenchman as he leaves our house. We make eye contact but he doesn't slow down.

The wooden box is on the kitchen worktop. Walnut with brass fittings. My wife stands over it, serene to the point of glowing.

"Someone's spent our savings," I say.

She smiles distantly as though theft is of no interest to her. "My mum," she says.

"Your mum spent our money?"

"My mum has been returned to me."

"Her ashes?"

"Her spirit." She touches the box. "It's called a Boîte Fantôme."

"Your mum was a big woman. I don't think she'd fit in there."

"Silly," says my wife. "Her body was big but we burned that."

"And now she's in the box?"

"It was worth every penny."

The Frenchman is a fraud. He's sold my wife a substitute mother for the sum of our savings. I try to reason with her. I tell her she needs to get our money back. I want her to open the box so she can see it's empty.

"Silly," she says. "If I open the box, Mum will escape."

I cancel our holiday because we don't have the money to pay for it anymore. When the tumble dryer dies, we can't afford a new one. My wife doesn't care. Everywhere she goes, she carries the box with her. She empties the contents of her handbag until it sort-of fits. At night, she keeps it on her bedside table. The one time we try to have sex, I can't relax. I can feel the box watching me.

That's when I decide to call Shaun.

I blame a lot of things on the fact I married too young. The crappy job I never quit. My unfulfilled desire to backpack around the world. And Shaun.

Shaun and I had been dating for three months when my mother-in-law saw us together. We were leaving a hotel, holding hands. When she asked me about it, my fumbled lie might as well have been a full confession. I sat in my car, inventing excuses, certain she was going to tell my wife, but I needn't have bothered. The following afternoon, my mother-in-law collapsed on the steps of her church and never regained consciousness.

In bed, Shaun rolls over to ask me about the Boîte Fantôme. I tell him about my mother-in-law's funeral and how the Frenchman exploited my wife. "You have to open the box," he says. "You need to set your mother-in-law free."

I can't believe he thinks she's in there—he's as bad my wife—but he makes a good point. Whether she's in there or not, opening the box is the right thing to do.

I wait until my wife's in the shower and then search the house. The box isn't on her bedside table. It isn't in her handbag. It isn't on the stacking tables opposite the television. Maybe she's come to her senses and seen it for what it is. No magic, no ghosts, just a wooden box designed to separate the grieving from their cash. I search every room in the house until there's only one left.

My wife is singing in the shower as I press open the bathroom door. The Boîte Fantôme is on the toilet. I sneak in and hope the steam on the shower doors will hide me.

"What are you doing?"

Before she can stop me, I seize the box and lift the lid. There's no sound, no movement, just an empty box and a wife who wants to kill me.

The following morning, I wake up in the spare room and creak downstairs to make a cup of tea. The kettle is empty and so is the water jug. I step back, confused, because I'm sure I filled the jug before I went to bed. I check the cutlery drawer and there are knives where there should be spoons; forks where there should be knives.

Someone wants me to think my mother-in-law has come back.

I hear voices in the main bedroom. My wife and somebody else. I race upstairs and barge through the door, expecting to find my wife with her conspirator, laughing at the trick they've played on me. But my wife's alone.

"Who were you talking to?" I ask.

She stares at me, shaking, her eyes brimming with sorrow. "My mum," she says. "My mum was here."

And I know what's coming. I can hear the question before it reaches my wife's lips.

"Who's Shaun?"

LINGERING

The house is perfectly still. Post pokes through the letter box and a single pair of shoes is missing from the rack by the front door. There's a breakfast bowl and a half-drunk mug of coffee next to the sink. Everything else is tidy.

"Where are you, Mummy?" calls Jacob from his bedroom.

While the rest of the world is at work, I'm in the living room, curled up on the sofa with a blanket over my legs. Until a month ago, my job was to interpret the data outputs from the Large Hadron Collider in Geneva. I can still remember the look on my boss's face when I told him I wasn't coming back. "What will you do?" he asked. It was an impossible question. "I don't know," I replied. "Science isn't the solution it used to be."

Upstairs, Jacob calls for me again.

I remember, fondly, the chaos of his hair first thing in the morning. The soft skin of his hand when it slipped unexpectedly into mine. The way I felt when he said, "Love you, Mummy." I want to go up to his room but I'm afraid of what I might find.

In the living room, I search for distractions—anything for a moment's respite—but the television is off and there's a spider on the opposite wall that's been there so long I've named it. I'm distantly aware of keys turning in a lock and the front door opening. My husband, Mark, arrives in his pin-stripe suit with a rucksack slung over his shoulder.

"Honey?" he says.

I stare at the wall, clinging to it like the motionless spider. I wonder: when spiders die, do they fall off? Or do they linger like a stain from the past?

"How's your day been?" asks Mark. Ordinary words, casual interest. I'm quite sure he's talking to me as if I'm one of his patients. Somewhere, deep inside, I know he's moving on.

***

It was snowing when we took Jacob to the hospital. The sky swarmed with puffs of white and I couldn't walk without slipping on the pavement. I wanted to hold Jacob's hand but I didn't dare in case I fell and pulled him over. And I did fall over, more than once, landing on my bum in the slush at the edge of the road. Jacob laughed so hard he got hiccups, and I suppose I laughed too. In those moments, I forgot he was sick. An hour later, the oncologist said it was only a matter of time.

I should have been there at the end but a faulty connection in the collider caused several tonnes of liquid helium to vent in an explosion that was heard for miles. My boss left a dozen messages for me, increasingly frantic, urging me to come to work. In the hospital carpark, Mark pleaded with me as I climbed into my car, asking "What's more important than our son?" The answer, of course, was nothing. Somehow, I'd convinced myself that Jacob would wait, that he wouldn't die if I wasn't there. I drove away, the windscreen wipers useless against my tears.

***

In the living room, I retreat behind a wall of resentment. "You don't hear him," I say. "You don't hear his suffering. His loneliness. He doesn't even call to you." I know I'm not being reasonable. Mark was there when Jacob died and I wasn't. There's no logic to my hostility but this isn't a matter of science anymore. Yes, science is capable of cruelty, it's fundamental for food chains and evolution. Stars die to make life possible. But science is impartial; wherever there is cruelty, there is purpose. What's happening to me, in my home, can't be explained by dark matter or superstring theory.

It's just mean.

"Laura?" says Mark. His tone is more urgent now. He rushes across the room, drops to his knees and presses his fingers against the side of my neck.

***

Jacob was waiting for me when I arrived home from his funeral, his little voice bouncing down the stairs like a lost ball. I sent Mark up to investigate, saying I thought I'd heard a bird or a cat, but of course he found nothing. "It's an old house," he said. "There are always noises." Days passed before I was brave enough to enter Jacob's bedroom. When I did, I was met with silence. The air was thick with dust and memories. I wept into my sleeves and begged my son to come back to me. Jacob didn't answer until I was downstairs again.

Determined to prove he was still in the house, I returned to what I knew best. I installed video monitors, motion sensors, thermometers, and a full spectrum HD camcorder so I could monitor his room throughout the day. With every negative result, I felt more certain he was there, hiding from me. The absence of evidence was evidence in itself. And then I captured an audio recording of his voice. I listened to it on repeat while I waited for Mark to return home. When I played it for him, he said he couldn't hear anything. The wave data was inconclusive.

There was only one experiment left to try. I emptied the bottle of sleeping pills onto the kitchen worktop and poured myself a large glass of vodka.

***

I thought I'd be braver in death. For hours now, I've been sitting on the sofa, watching dust particles collide without consequence and trying to find the will to move.

Mark's sobbing into my lap. I want to run my fingers through his hair, to reassure him that it's okay because I'm going to see our precious little boy again just as soon as I go upstairs.

But I can't.

I can't go upstairs.

Because what if I'm wrong?

SACK OF SOULS

He's there for the young man who immolates himself on the steps of the Cenotaph. He's there for the hundreds of terrified refugees whose dinghies capsize in the choppy waters of the Mediterranean. He waits behind the curtain of every flu and cancer victim. For the falls and suicides, the road traffic accidents and state sanctioned murders, he lingers in the shadows with his hessian sack held ready. His sack has never felt so heavy.

In Southern Nevada he attends a Gamblers Anonymous meeting. No one asks for his name and he doesn't wear a badge, choosing instead to sit alone at the back of the room and sip sherry from a flask. After the meeting, when everyone else has left, he steps up to the podium, sweeps his beard to one side and leans towards the microphone. "I have a problem," he says in a solemn baritone. "I like to gamble. Card games mostly. Tarock, Tarocco; anything with Tarot cards." His voice catching, he says "I gambled everything I had. My passion, my purpose, everything. I lost."

In his shades-of-black suit, he's there when the plane crashes in the Indian Ocean, for the gun massacre in Ohio and the starving children in the Sudan. His sack, which was once filled with the promise of joy, now bulges and throbs like a diseased heart.

He finds Jenny sitting on a bench in Castle Park, staring up through the freezing mist to the ruins of St Peter's Church. She wears the mismatched threads of the homeless and cradles a can of super-strength lager in the crook of her arm. He sits next to her and sips his sherry.

"Stuff'll kill you," she says.

He spits the sherry back into the flask. It's been fifty years since someone acknowledged his presence. He tucks the flask away in the folds of his suit and leans closer to her. Like so many bench dwellers, she wears a heady perfume of sweat and piss and tobacco. And even when she speaks, she hardly moves at all.

"If you were hoping for a kiss," she says, "you're shit outta luck."

He can't help but laugh. She reminds him of the little girl who spoke to him fifty years ago, the one whose eyes shone like baubles on a tree. She demanded to see inside his sack in case there was something she wanted more than the presents he'd already left at the foot of her bed. When he refused, she folded her arms and scowled.

On the bench, Jenny says "We've met before, haven't we?" Her eyes sparkle when they catch the moonlight. Then she coughs and it's a violent reflex that tears deep into her chest. A thin line of spittle and blood connects her bottom lip to the frost-speckled concrete below. Carefully, he touches his hand to her shoulder.

"Last time I saw you," she croaks, "you were wearing red. You were happier then."

He helps her to lie down on the bench, her frail body seeming to collapse inside her sleeping bag. There are other places he's supposed to be but they can wait. Boats will sink and schools will burn, but how long will it be before he meets another Jenny?

"I lost everything, too," she says.

"One thing I've learned," he replies, "you can't cheat Death." He kisses her on the forehead and whispers "You can see inside my sack now."

As Jenny's spirit leaves her body, a sleigh passes overhead, pulled by a dozen hooved and snarling animals. It's filled with presents wrapped in every colour of the season, anchored in place by the blade of a scythe. The sleigh's rider holds onto the reins with long, bony fingers; a pack of Tarot cards tucked up one sleeve and a smile permanently carved into his face.

For any children who are still awake when their presents are delivered, Christmas will never be the same again.

BAUBLES & BEER CANS

John waters the dead poinsettias and retrieves his wife's present from its hiding place on top of the kitchen units. Every Christmas for a lifetime they've competed to give each other the most thoughtful gift and usually his wife wins.

But this year he's found something special.

'I'm just making a cup of coffee for you, my love,' he calls up the stairs. He's startled by his reflection in the shiny mirror of the kettle. Thin lips and bulging eyes. Ears that have never stopped growing. Like a faded photograph, his skin is nearly as white as his hair, making him seem incorporeal and ghostlike. He doesn't care anymore. Youth is for other people; he's quite at home in his old age.

The mug tree is bare and the only cups on the cluttered worktops are furry with mould. His wife's always nagging him to wash up but the dishcloth is lost in the sink, buried beneath a tower of crockery, and there's a thick scum the colour of brandy butter floating on the water.

John places the present on the kitchen worktop and tears off strips of sticky tape, lining them up like sprinters at the start of a race. He can't remember where he put the wrapping paper but the front cover of the local newspaper features a picture of a Christmas tree surrounded by smiling school kids. It's perfect.

'Just washing up some mugs,' he says.

The walls of their house are dotted with photographs, a tribute to his wife's lifelong hobby. Sand- and sun-filled holidays, and wine-drenched family gatherings, all captured on shiny photographic paper and squeezed into ever-shrinking islands of bare wall. There are memories everywhere but he rarely stops to look. He's worried he'll find himself lost in the past.

In the living room, the Christmas tree shimmers like a house fire. He decorated it himself this year and it's a triumph of timeless classics and creative substitutes: baubles and beer cans, tinsel and utensils, and strings of lights that unwind through the decades. It's the best tree he's ever seen.

'Won't be long now,' he says.

He remembers when the lounge belonged to Samantha, their frenetic and seemingly inexhaustible puppy, who chewed the furniture and made them feel young again. On top of the television is a photo of a weary-eyed Labrador in her final days. What he'd give to spend one more Christmas with her, watching her chase the rabbits along the riverside. But you can't get them back once they're gone.

He finds a pen on the coffee table, amongst magazines of half-finished crosswords, and returns to the kitchen to write the label for his wife's present. She's going to be so surprised. It's their wedding photo, the one of them standing in sunshine outside the church, smiling in a blizzard of confetti. She looked so beautiful in her wedding dress. So perfectly happy. The photo went missing when they downsized nearly three decades ago and neither of them thought they'd ever see it again. Then he found it in the attic, at the bottom of a box of curtains, where his wife had put it to keep it safe when they moved.

The steaming kettle calls him back to the present. He retrieves a couple of camping mugs from a forgotten picnic hamper, a Christmas present from a long-dead relative. The teaspoon rattles in the sugar bowl as he carries the tray upstairs. His wife's bedside table is covered with untouched drinks but that's okay. Last Christmas she was in hospital, her body so frail they said she might never leave. This year it doesn't matter that she won't get out of bed. It doesn't matter that her smile looks more like a grimace, or that her eyes refuse to blink. It's enough to have her home.

He opens the window to let in some fresh air, rests the tray on the dresser and wishes her a merry Christmas.

AUTHOR NOTES

Don't read this section. If you've enjoyed the stories in this collection, why not quit while you're ahead? And if it hasn't captured your imagination so far, these nuggets of needless self-indulgence probably aren't going to change your mind. So put the book back on the shelf and keep an eye on your neighbours. Clean your golf clubs and barbeque the rug. And wash those clothes on an eco-friendly cycle before it's too late.

Or…

If you're one of those people who likes to know a little bit more about the stories you've read—about where they come from and why—you might find something of interest in the notes that follow. And if you're one of those people who, like me, can't put a book down until they've consumed every word, pour yourself another cup of tea and make yourself comfortable, because this is for you.

"Norfolk"—I used to drive my eldest son to Norfolk late at night, so we could prepare the family bungalow for when Holly and the twins arrived the following day. Virtually all of Eccles was lost to the sea during a storm hundreds of years ago, and today not much is left apart from the small collection of bungalows that make up the Bush Estate. As a kid visiting Eccles with my parents, I remember seeing the partial ruins of the original church tower exposed on the beach. Thankfully I've never stumbled across any skeletons from the old graveyard, although there are stories of this happening. It's always best to check before sending the kids over to play in the sea—you never know what they'll find.

"Whistle-stop"—the oldest story in this collection, and one of the first I ever had published, was written for the pop culture issue of *Yellow Chair Review*. They wanted stories about 80s arcade games, and I couldn't resist writing one about a boy with an unusual approach to playing (or not). The rest of the story is based on a driving holiday I took with Holly before the boys were born. We really did sing to the bears as we hiked through the woods to watch salmon jumping up the rapids. And the local Pinot Noir is as good as any I've tasted.

"Boleskine"—around the time I turned thirty, my sister and I drove to Scotland to spend the weekend camping near Loch Ness. It was a cold and drizzly weekend, and we spent about as much time on the road as we did by the loch. While we were there, we tried to lure the monster out of hiding by challenging it to a duel—*umbrellas at dawn*—figuring no one else would have been daft enough to try this approach. Sadly, the monster wasn't persuaded. While we were there, we stumbled across Boleskine House, the former home of Aleister Crowley, and I knew my stories would take me back there one day.

"Gettysburg"— I'd just put the twins to bed after a four-hour drive back from Norfolk when I received some news that would keep me awake all night. My phone pinging every few minutes as writer friends around the world acknowledged the news didn't help. I must have checked a dozen times to make sure the news was true, and every time it was there in black and white: I'd won The Molotov Cocktail's Flash Rage contest. Moments like this are why I write.

"Oymyakon"—Oymyakon is the coldest, permanently inhabited place in the world. The moment I came across it in a news story, I knew it was going to be the setting of a story. My original idea featured a thaw in the ice, during which prehistoric bugs escaped and made a home in the back of a television set. By altering the images on the screen, they were able to hypnotise the owners of the television set, who went out to the ice to liberate more prehistoric creatures. I know—it sounds like the plot for an abandoned episode of the X-files. I've learned the hard way that it doesn't always pay to write the first idea that comes into my head. But I love how this one turned out and it's the first story I sold to The Arcanist.

"Children of the Moon"—I grew up watching horror movies like Poltergeist, Fright Night, and An American Werewolf in London, but the coolest of them all was undoubtedly The Lost Boys. I still love the soundtrack. At fifteen, I dreamt up a short story called 'The Chenwick Children', inspired by The Lost Boys, about a vampire who settles in a sleepy seaside town, only to find the children there have a dark secret of their own. I never wrote the story but I never forgot the idea. When ZeroFlash asked for 80s-themed horror stories, I finally had the opportunity to lay that old vampire to rest.

"Jeremy's Wish"—there's something wickedly satisfying about this Oedipus-by-proxy tale. Every Christmas I'm terrified my boys are going to reject their presents and take it out on me in some horribly creative way.

"Heart of Stone"—I wrote the original draft of this story in a single sitting. I knew it was missing something, but I didn't know what, so I filed it away and forgot about it. More than a year later, I stumbled across the story again and was particularly taken with the 'balled-up sock' description. This is a new version of the story, where that line is perhaps the only thing that remains from the original.

"Little Black Holes"—I was driving home from the hospital, following a consultation about the removal of a benign tumour from my thumb, when I had the idea for this story. It was a fiercely hot day and, as I was driving, I noticed how deep the shadows were on the road. Like the characters in the story, I just kept staring and staring. The first draft didn't take long to write but it took me ages to find my way to a finished draft. In the meantime, this story was rejected—a *lot*. And then Cease, Cows kindly published it and the story made the Wigleaf longlist, as well as being nominated for a Pushcart Prize and BIFFY50. I love a happy ending, even if I don't write them very often.

"Another Side of Gustav Holst"—The thing that appealed to me most about this story was the chance to describe a landscape using mainly musical terms. It's not an opportunity that comes along every day. I'd wanted to write a story about a missing piece of music from The Planets suite for a while, and I couldn't resist this tale of academic squabbling and parallel dimensions.

"The Lamppost Huggers"—we were on holiday in France when I finished second in The Molotov Cocktail's 2018 Flash Monster contest. If I remember rightly, the kids got a special trip to Raptor Park with my winnings. The phrase 'Lamppost Huggers' had popped into my head one morning and I immediately wrote it down—knowing it was good but never suspecting it would one day be the title of my debut collection. Much of the rest of the story was inspired by the many years I spent queueing at the bus stop on my way to work.

"Two Weeks to Wolf"—this one was inspired by a news story about a wolf-like creature that was shot and killed by a farmer in Montana. If it wasn't a wolf, what was it? That's the question pondered by the characters in this story. I never found out the outcome of the real-life shooting—probably because the mystery was more newsworthy than the facts. I wonder if they considered the answer proposed by the narrator of this story?

"Fledglings"—when The Arcanist announced their Monster Flash contest, I trawled through my archives, looking for inspiration. Eventually I stumbled across the first sentence of this story. It was sitting there, on its own at the top of a page, as if it had been waiting for me. I relocated my laptop to the back garden, sat down and wrote, with no idea of how the story was going to unfold. "Fledglings" was the result. I'm still amazed it won the contest, and I'm very grateful it resulted in this collection.

"Weather Cycle"—this is a new story, published here for the first time. In Kathy Fish's opening session at the 2019 Flash Fiction Festival, she got us all to write a story against the clock while she threw words and phrases at us. There are writers out there who create amazing works of art under these conditions—stories that will make you laugh and cry and quite possibly quit writing—but I'm not one of them. I can't remember the story I wrote but I do remember it had a washing machine in it. And there was something curious about that washing machine. Something that made me want to look closer...

"Endangered"—my first ever prize-winning story was inspired by a wonderful and deeply upsetting photo taken by British wildlife photographer, Andy Rouse. The photo is of a penguin chick surrounded by hungry caracaras, and I've never forgotten it. Originally, this story was going to be much longer, with mankind calling upon an advanced alien civilisation for help in a last, desperate attempt to save the planet. The spaceships arrived, but only to watch and wait while we destroyed ourselves. I think the published version of the story works much better. Although spaceships are cool, too.

"And the World Roared Back"—was originally going to be a two-minute script for a community film about the end of the world. I never wrote the script. Instead, I turned the story into a flash, which found a home in the debut issue of The Green Light. Interestingly, once the film scripts were in, the producers bemoaned the lack of stories featuring children. Maybe I missed my calling…

"Lepidoptera"—I'd been bouncing this idea around since Holly and I first moved in together. Originally it was going to be a short story called 'Hey, Joe' about vampires who market themselves as 'a solution for modern living', and how they don't need to be invited into modern, mass-produced homes because 'the buildings have no soul.' I'm glad I never finished the short story—the voice in the flash fiction version is much more sinister.

"Under a Black Glass Ceiling"—this was going to be one of the previously unpublished stories in this collection. And it would have been, if Steve Campbell from Ellipsis Zine hadn't reached out to ask if I had anything he could publish over Halloween in 2019. How could I say no? I'm not sure where the idea came from— but since the kids have been born, Holly and I hardly ever get to eat out at fancy restaurants, so it probably has something to do with that.

"Sack of Souls"—more years ago that I'd care to count, I won a school writing competition with a story that featured the characters of Santa and Death battling over the life of a sick boy. I can't remember what it was called, but I do remember that I wrote the Santa sections in a comedy style that attempted to emulate Terry Pratchett, and the Death sections in a horror style inspired by James Herbert. I never expected for Santa and Death to meet again in my fiction but here they are in one of my darkest stories, where Death has already played the winning hand.

"Baubles and Beer Cans"—the original version of this story, 'Christmas Morning', was my first ever shortlisting in a competition—the inaugural Inktears flash fiction competition to be precise. It took me several more rewrites before I found the right voice to properly tell the story. It's another dark one—what is it about Christmas that inspires such horrors?

So that's it. These are the stories behind the stories in the collection, and now it's time to move on to new things. And who knows? Maybe there'll be a few more flash fictions further down the road. Until then, thanks for reading. May your nightmares be brutal and swift.

PUBLISHING NOTES

This collection probably wouldn't exist without the incredible work done by the following journals and associated editors, who have kindly championed my stories over the past five years:

"Foreword" (as "Run, Child") first appeared in *Quantum Fairy Tales #18*, 2016

"Norfolk" first appeared in *Twisted Tales 2016*, Annie Evett & Margie Riley (ed.), published by Raging Aardvark Publishing, 2016 (runner-up, Twisted Tales contest)

"Whistle-stop" (as "Whistler") first appeared *Yellow Chair Review*, 2015

"Boleskine" first appeared in *The Molotov Cocktail*, 2016

"Gettysburg" first appeared in *The Molotov Cocktail* 2017 (winner, Flash Rage contest)

"Absent Spouse Syndrome" first appeared in *The Green Light*, 2017

"Oymyakon" first appeared in *The Arcanist*, 2018

"Children of the Moon" first appeared in *ZeroFlash,* 2017

"Jeremy's Wish" first appeared in *The Arcanist*, 2018

"Heart of Stone" – previously unpublished

"Wicked Collaboration" first appeared in *Trickster's Treats #2: More Tales from the Pumpkin Patch*, Steve Dillon (ed.), published by Things in the Well, 2018

"Little Black Holes" first appeared in *Cease, Cows*, 2018

"Worry Dragons" (as "The Worry Dragons") first appeared in *Twisted Sister Lit Mag*, 2017

"Another Side of Gustav Holst" first appeared in *Unnerving Magazine #9*, Eddie Generous (ed.), 2018

"The Lamppost Huggers" first appeared in *The Molotov Cocktail*, 2018 (runner-up, Flash Monster contest)

"Two Weeks to Wolf" first appeared in *Aphotic Realm Magazine #6 'Fangs'*, Dustin Schyler Yoak, A. A. Medina & Chris Martin (ed.), 2019

"Fledglings" first appeared in *Monster Flash*, Josh Hrala, Andie Fullmer & Patrick Morris (ed.), published by The Arcanist, 2019 (winner, Monster Flash contest)

"Weather Cycle" – previously unpublished

"Summer Snow" – previously unpublished

"Endangered" first appeared in *The Short Story*, 2016 (winner, monthly contest)

"And the World Roared Back" first appeared in *The Green Light*, 2017

"Lepidoptera" first appeared in *The Arcanist,* 2018

"Under a Black Glass Ceiling" first appeared in *Ellipsis Zine*, 2019

"Boîte Fantôme" first appeared in *Ghost Stories*, Josh Hrala, Andie Fullmer & Patrick Morris (ed.), published by The Arcanist, 2018 (winner, Ghost Stories contest)

"Lingering" first appeared in *The Arcanist*, 2019

"Sack of Souls" first appeared in *The Molotov Cocktail*, 2016

"Baubles & Beer Cans" first appeared in *Shades of Santa: Tales from the Bloody North Pole*, Steve Dillon (ed.), published by Things in the Well, 2017

ACKNOWLEDGEMENTS

What collection of horrors would be complete without a little finger pointing to finish things off? Firstly, I must thank Josh, Andie and Patrick at The Arcanist for believing in this project and making this writer's lifelong dream come true. It's been a pleasure working with you—although I fear you did most of the work, while I had all the fun.

Thank you also to those kindly souls who read and provided feedback on these stories before I set them loose on the world. We all know there's a fine line between success and the *other thing*, and I do believe you've nudged me across it many times. I won't attempt to name you all—there have been a few—but Richie Brown, Emily Harrison, and my friends at the Bath Company of Writers have been there for the moments that matter. I can't tell you how much I appreciate knowing I'm not alone.

Next, I must mention Kealan Patrick Burke who provided the amazing artwork for the cover. For what it's worth, I loved every iteration.

To all my friends in Team Darkness, including Josh and Mary at The Molotov Cocktail, and Christina who wrote the fantastic introduction for this collection, you rock and you know it.

Finally, no journey would be complete without a few family visits along the way. I'd like to thank my mum, dad and sister for never giving up on me. It feels like you've wanted me to be a writer since I first picked up a pen, and here we are. And to Holly (my wife), and Dylan, Charlie and Oscar (my sons)—thank you for giving me the longest list of reasons not to spend my life at the keyboard. Don't ever underestimate how important this is. I love you all.

Christopher Stanley
Bristol, England
January, 2020

ABOUT THE AUTHOR

Christopher Stanley lives on a hill in England with three sons who share a birthday but aren't triplets. He is the author of the novelette, The Forest is Hungry (published by Demain Publishing), and the short story, Suds & Monsters, which was selected from over 800 stories to be the opening story in The Third Corona Book of Horror Stories.

When he's not hugging lampposts, Christopher can be found lurking in the shadowy corners of Twitter @allthosestrings, or looking for inspiration amongst the many splendid shelves of Goodreads.

MORE FROM
CHRISTOPHER STANLEY

READ
MORE
FLASH
FICTION

www.TheArcanist.io